HUNT FOR THE MYSTERIOUS EYE

By the Same Author

The Girl in the House

Born to Dream

HUNT FOR THE MYSTERIOUS EYE

HARSHVARDHAN RAO

Srishti
Publishers & Distributors

Srishti Publishers & Distributors
A unit of AJR Publishing LLP
212A, Peacock Lane
Shahpur Jat, New Delhi – 110 049

editorial@srishtipublishers.com

First published by
Srishti Publishers & Distributors in 2024

10 9 8 7 6 5 4 3 2 1

Printed and bound in India

Contents

Preface

Speaking of the number '24', what comes to your mind? A day with 24 hours? But the number 24 has much more significance. In our world, the number 24 has a more profound meaning.

In our body, we have 24 ribs that connect to our backbone. The Ashok Chakra has 24 spokes representing Buddha's teachings about the intricate connections in life – how things lead to other things. The first 12 spokes show how suffering unfolds, while the following 12 point to a realm beyond simple cause and effect.

In Hindu mythology, in Treta Yug, Lord Vishnu appeared on earth as Lord Rama 24 different times in 24 forms. Ratnakar, once a notorious robber, changed his path to become Maharishi Valmiki, known as the 'Adikavi' or the first poet. His great work, the *Ramayana,* has 24 thousand shlokas or verses. When the first word of each shloka is put in the sequence, it forms the syllables of Gayatri Mantra – 24 syllables.

This book has 24 chapters that dive into 24 pieces that keep hunting for a mystery. It's a tale of a treasure hunt that includes friendship, betrayal, love, belief, promise, and hunger for power.

Before you go any further, I want to leave you with a knowledge about a unique medical condition called face blindness. Have you heard about it?

Face blindness, also known as Prosopagnosia1, is an impairment in the recognition of facial identity. Prosopagnosics[1] often have difficulty recognizing family members, close friends, and even themselves. They

---

1 https://www.faceblind.org/research/#:~:text=Prosopagnosia%2C%20also%20called%20face%20blindness,as%20recognition%20via%20the%20face.

tend to use alternative routes to recognition, but these routes are not as effective as recognition via the face.

Prologue

For thousands of years, people of many faiths have worshiped relics. The Kinglas are not an exception. The Kinglas pray to a mysterious object which has a unique resonance. Members of today's secret society of Kinglas have pinned their hopes and prayers on this object. This object was blessed to the founding fathers of the Kingla secret society to save them from death and show them a path to always give back to society. Giving back to society and the people were the true reasons for the secret society's existence and this object guided them towards this path.

Why was this object so powerful?

This mysterious object was like opening a secret society member's heart in front of him. It made them feel connected with their roots, and truly understand what their purpose in life as secret society members was. This object certainly performed miracles to keep the secret society together united in cohesion.

The origin of this mysterious object has been cloaked in mystery. And that particular day that occurs twice every year was the day when members of the secret society will witness this mysterious object and feel connected to the cosmic energy that it radiates. Some believe it is so powerful that they liken it to God coming down and touching them.

But little did they know that the mysterious object, the relic, is going be stolen soon from the secret society. And to be gone forever!

Chapter 1

Agha Netra – The Birth

Sometime around late 4th century BCE

The oil lamps lit up the room, engulfing it in its yellow warmth. But the anxiousness among the nine men was clearly palpable. These men had been handpicked to protect something which had the power to change the fate of the king and the empire. And that object of mystery was about to be delivered at any moment.

Suddenly, the sound of hurrying footsteps could be heard in the hallway. With each passing second, the sound became louder. Every increase in the decibel of footsteps multiplied their worry many folds. Suddenly, the sound stopped, and all the nine darted their eyes towards the door. A man holding a box was panting heavily. He stretched his hand holding out the box towards the nine, and fainted. All of them rushed to pick him up, but one hand reached for the box, which had fallen a few feet away from the man. The box was the size of a book, brown in colour and with a picture of an eye engraved finely in its centre. A peculiar hue of red colour was being emitted from the eye. It was so hypnotic that the one holding the box could keep looking at it for hours.

Then one man looked at the box, picked it up, and murmured, "Are we keeping this thing away from Magadh King?"

The remaining eight came closer to look at the box and left the man lying unconscious on the floor. Surrounding the box, they chorused, "Agha Netra!"

"Shall we open it?" a man said, his voice trembling.

Suddenly, a loud voice knifed the silence in the room.

"No one should open the Agha Netra!"

All the nine gathered around the Agha Netra like a flock, looked in the direction of the voice. A mysterious man stood in the shadows. He was wearing a black robe and his face was hidden inside the hood.

"You are the nine chosen by the King himself to protect the Agha Netra. It is not to be opened till eternity. You are the nine protectors. This box holds a secret location in a Lipi where the King has buried his blood-drenched weapons. The secret place also houses the cursed treasures that the King has gathered from the wars he fought and won. It is estimated that the treasure is enough to feed the Maurya Empire for an entire decade. The Lipi, which has the location, is secured inside the Agha Netra."

The man paused and walked up. He sat on the seat made of rock.

He looked at the herd of nine.

"The King is leaving everything and starting his journey in search of moksha. But in this journey, even the sight of any evil weapon and or the treasure, might make him return to a blood-thirsty war. The Agha Netra has an evil eye that can see everything. The only way to keep it safe from the world is to hide it by protecting it. It should be eternally protected by all nine of you. The only way to leave this group of nine is through death. But if someone dies, then it is the responsibility of the others to fill that gap. One among you will be the messenger of Agha Netra, who has the power to describe the the Agha Netra to the person who will replace the missing man. And you should select that messenger among yourselves."

The nine pairs of eyes stared at the one-eyed Agha Netra. And all were more terrified when they came to know that they were looking at a mighty devil; it could create unimaginable destruction to humanity if it were to be in the possession of another human. One of them looked towards the rock, and to his surprise, the knight was gone. He had vanished into thin air. They knew the mysterious man had come as a messenger to remind the nine chosen ones of what they possessed and what they were responsible for.

That was the moment when the first group of nine men were formed and to protect the Agha Netra for eternity.

Chapter 2

In Safe Hands

In the year 1857, in Barrackpore in the eastern part of India, a sepoy mutiny was being kindled to light the first fire of the freedom struggle. At the same time, the old tradition of finding a replacement for a member of the Agha Netra was taking place near Kalighat. Eravanth was one of the nine members of the protectors of the Agha Netra who had died of cholera that year. And the protectors couldn't be less than nine. So they immediately needed to find a suitable replacement.

At midnight, Kalighat was quiet and dark. The light emitting from the small diyas was not bright enough, however, there was not enough wind to extinguish that tiny dot. Near the banks of the river, a few dark and tall figures could be seen walking towards the north entrance of the temple. One was short and lean compared to the rest and could easily be marked as the odd one out. They were all nine. The Unknowns. They gathered and lit a bonfire on the main veranda. The small figure walked towards the bonfire and stood beside it as the rest stood in the dark. They were audible, but not visible to him.

"It was hard to find a replacement for Eravanth; you were the only chosen one."

One voice could be heard from the dark.

"As far as our memory goes, we don't remember anyone's son ever becoming the next Unknown to protect the Agha Netra."

"Are you sure he is Eravanth's son? He doesn't look like us," another voice interrupted.

"He is Eravanth's son, Arinjay. His mother was from Xiamen in China," the first one replied.

"Xiamen!" another voice exclaimed from the dark.

"You know very well that Wo Shing Wo is looking for the Agha Netra. Does Arinjay have any Xiamen connection?"

"No, he was born here in the north. The son of this soil with no connection to Xiamen," the first voice replied.

A figure walked into the light of the bonfire. He was wearing a long black robe with a hood over his head. He stood close to Arinjay, went down on his knees, and looked up at him.

"Son, I am Namish Sarkar." He put his hand in his pocket and took out a brown box and showed it to him, and continued.

"This is the Agha Netra. Since Magadh King created the Nine Unknowns to spread his knowledge, there have been other Nine Unknowns who were given the duty of protecting the mysterious Agha Netra. We, the Eight Unknowns, are continuing this tradition to keep the Nine intact to protect it. These Nine were called the protectors, who are now us. We are Unknowns to the outside world. There is always one messenger who can communicate about the Agha Netra. As a messenger, I have been chosen by the other eight, obviously including Eravanth, when he was alive. You must be wondering what is inside the Agha Netra, and why are we protecting it? You will only come to know that later, during this journey of safeguarding and keeping it a secret from the world. Hidden."

He took a deep breath, paused, and continued, "Listen, son, we have to protect it. Promise us; it will not go to Wo Shing Wo at any cost."

Arinjay looked into Namish's eyes. They were big and shiny, and the bonfire's reflection was easily visible in his eyes, like fire in his eyes in search of its true protector. Arinjay was mesmerized, but there was not a single expression on his face that showed Arinjay that he was completely taken in by Namish. With a poker face, Arinjay nodded his head and said,

"Not till I am alive!"

Namish smiled and said, "Let me tell you this, son, as you are also one of the protectors. Remember one thing: when the devil leaves you, you have done something wrong because his work is done through you as a medium. But the devil comes at you when you are doing something right. Watch out for what you are doing, not for the devil. Protect the Agha Netra."

Arinjay nodded his head again. Then he looked around, and he saw that all the figures around the bonfire were gone. They had vanished without a trace. He turned back to Namish; he was gone too. Worrying, he looked at the floor, and he saw something scribbled on it.

'Swagamah' (स्वागमः) which meant 'welcome.'

The Agha Netra triad had dispersed, and Arinjay was inducted as the ninth member of the protectors of the Agha Netra.

Chapter 3

Poverty a Devil

Arinjay left Kalighat temple with the responsibility of protecting the Agha Netra. Being a protector added to his existing responsibility of fighting the battle against poverty. He had gone to Kalighat hoping to ask the other eight men for financial help, but before he could even broach the topic, they were gone, leaving Arinjay alone.

Arinjay took a week to reach home, where his widowed mother was waiting for him. He arrived home empty-handed with only a promise. His mother had realized early on that Eravanth's honesty and loyalty to protect the Agha Netra brought no rewards; not a single penny.

"We should move back to Xiamen to my brother's house; there is nothing for us here." His mother looked at Arinjay with wet eyes.

"I have promised them that I will protect Agha Netra till I am alive," Arinjay said with a frown.

"You have to be alive to protect the Agha Netra. Will that promise give us money, food, or shelter? Can that promise protect us so that you, in turn, can protect the Agha Netra? No, my son, your father has done enough, and he got nothing in return. You have your life in front of you. Let's not waste it here," his mother cried.

"Bu—" Arinjay said, but he was cut short.

"We can never rise from poverty if we let it become our normal. If we accept this fact today, we will remain in its grip our whole life."

She paused and continued, "I won't listen to you. We need to pack our bags and leave," she replied with authority.

Arinjay has seen his mother's pain in the past but was unable to help her. And now, her stubbornness to move to Xiamen was something he couldn't oppose.

Arinjay said with a determined look, "You have to promise me one thing. In Xiamen you will not tell anyone that I am protecting the Agha Netra. The day I get to know that you have revealed this secret, I will leave. My loyalty and love weigh equal in my life."

His mother nodded her head. They had almost a month to wrap up the house and move to Xiamen. Arinjay and his mother decided to gather all the used items from their house and sell them in the city market in return for money to migrate to Xiamen.

***

The war of independence was gearing up. The revolutionaries were growing steadily in number and were keen to see India as an independent nation. The aggression in Mussoorie was rising too. Recently there was news of a fatal attack on the British sergeant in Mussoorie, which was acting as fuel to ignite the minds of the young to join the fight for independence. Britishers were searching for suspected revolutionaries in every nook and corner to curb the craze among the young to join the freedom struggle.

Arinjay was not untouched by the feverish enthusiasm around him. He wanted to join hands, but the shackles of poverty had always kept him at bay from the freedom movement. That particular day, he was sitting at his house collecting old items to sell at the market. Suddenly, Arinjay heard a thud, and someone rushed inside his house, smashing the main door. Arinjay turned around in shock and saw a terrified Indian man inside his home. The man was panting and was drenched in sweat. He looked at Arinjay and shouted, punching his hand in the air,

"Long live India!"

Arinjay looked at him and slightly moved his hand in the air.

"The sepoys are searching for me. They will reach this house anytime. Please hide me somewhere. I need to send one message to Calcutta; I must remain alive. Please hide me somewhere... please," he pleaded.

Arinjay, in shock, stood frozen like stone looking at him. It was the first time he had seen a revolutionary so close. The man repeated himself, "Please save me. I will do anything for you. My life will be in your debt."

Arinjay pointed his hand towards the wardrobe, which was empty, as he had taken all the things out to sell.

In a heartbeat, the man jumped into the wardrobe. After a few minutes, the British soldiers came rushing into his house. They started to search relentlessly. A sergeant came close to Arinjay and asked in a commanding voice.

"Do you have any uninvited guests, my friend?"

Arinjay shivered at the loud and authoritative voice. He shook his head.

"Don't lie!" the sergeant shouted.

Arinjay trembled in fear. He again shook his head in disagreement.

"Understand. God forbid I find him in your house. I will also hang you with him in the middle of the goddamn road!" he threatened menacingly.

Arinjay said in a shaky voice,

"There is no one, sir."

Meanwhile, the soldiers searched the house. Luckily, they didn't think of checking the wardrobe.

The sergeant looked at Arinjay's soulful eyes and felt that he was telling the truth. He warned Arinjay not to hide anything and to pass on any information about the revolutionaries in case he learned anything.

Once they left the house, the man came out of the wardrobe.

"You have saved one freedom fighter today. I am indebted to you. If you need any help, you can ask people around Sylverton about me. My name is Arnab. They will tell you about me."

Arnab introduced himself and swiftly left the house, leaving Arinjay still in shock about what had just happened.

Chapter 4

Bespoke Duplicate Box

After a few days, Arinjay was sitting in the market with a few items from his home to sell. He was a naïve salesman. There was no specific spot allocated for him, so he searched for an empty area between the two shops. The shops were structures made of bamboo, which held up a thick cloth that acted as a canopy and provided some shade at the entrance. The walls were made up of a layer of soil slathered on the wall of big rock blocks. The walls between two shops were working as a coolant in the afternoon sun. Arinjay laid out the carpet to put his stuff to sell. Seeing a wet-behind-ear-kid, both the shopkeepers allowed him to put up his things.

Arinjay was in desperate need of money to arrange for his tickets to Xiamen in China. And he sat at his spot, waiting eagerly for customers. One day a man came up to him and asked for the price of a bag.

"How much for this bag?" the man asked.

"It is for two rupees," Arinjay replied.

"I don't have that much money, but I can give you something in exchange."

"I need money, sir; I am not interested in anything other than money," Arinjay said, ignoring the man and sat down on the carpet.

The man went close to Arinjay and looked at him. The eyes of the man had the same sparkle and fire that Arinjay has seen at Kalighat. It didn't take him a moment to realize that he was looking at the messenger.

"What you have got?" Arinjay replied in a shaking voice.

The man took out a box. It was the Agha Netra. He gave it to Arinjay. Then he held his hand, leaned towards him, and whispered in his ears.

"Protect it to prove your loyalty."

Then the man smiled, patted his back, and walked out of the scene. Arinjay looked at him helplessly. Yet again, he failed to ask for financial help.

Arinjay reached home with the Agha Netra. But he knew that he was breaking the promise he had given to the messenger. He knew that in Xiamen people were searching for the Agha Netra. The worst part was that he had the Agha Netra with him now. It would be impossible to protect it from Wo Shing Wo if Arinjay took the Agha Netra with him to Xiamen. The only way to protect it was by leaving it behind – safe, hidden, and unknown.

One day when Arinjay was in the market, he saw a carver working on a woodblock and carving a beautiful sculpture. It was of a woman carrying a child on her waist and holding a bundle on her head. The eyes of the woman seemed to be speaking words of inspiration about how she was not feeling the burden on her head because her baby was smiling. The hammer and chisel seemed to be singing a song together in creating the beautiful work of art. Looking at the carver and sculpture, something struck Arinjay; he took out the Agha Netra and went to him.

"This is beautiful; it feels like she will start breathing now," Arinjay said, looking at sculpture.

"She is already breathing and smiling; how beautifully the broken wood has turned into the graceful sculpture." The carver smiled at Arinjay.

"Tell me, son, what you want from me?" he continued.

Arinjay took out the Agha Netra and showed it to him.

"Can you replicate it?"

The carver looked at it and said, "I can re-create the box and the engraved image of that eye, but the inherited beauty the box carries can't be recreated. You will have a similar-looking box, but not the soul."

Arinjay smiled, as he knew that he was talking to the best carver he could find who could see and feel the Agha Netra.

"But I have to be around when you work. I will bring the box every day, you finish the work, and I will take it back with me," Arinjay told him.

"What is so special about this box, son?" the carver asked.

"If you ask me to give you something in life, I will provide you with the ability to see it through my eyes, and only then would you be able to realize how special this is to me." Arinjay paused and said, "This is the best way I can describe what is special about it."

"Looks like lost love is being remembered through the box," the carver chuckled.

"I don't think I am qualified to love someone so deeply. I have broken someone's trust and now I can't keep my promise," Arinjay smirked sadly.

For the next few days, Arinjay kept coming to the carver and waiting as he worked on the replica. Couple of days later, it was finally ready. It was the spitting-image of the Agha Netra. When the wooden boxes were kept next to each other, only Arinjay could spot the difference. The key was the faint hue coming out of the eye of the original.

Now, Arinjay had a plan to keep the box safe and protected from the world.

He had to find someone who could keep the Agha Netra with him without opening it. It had to be a person who was indebted to Arinjay and could be trusted.

Arinjay had a good day at the market as he sold a few of the items, earning enough to pay for the tickets, and get the replica ready. Finally, he reached home bone tired, and threw himself on his bed. As he relaxed, he pondered about who could keep the Agha Netra without opening it.

Chapter 5

Arnab and the Firearms

"Can we attain *swaraj* without weapons? Did I choose the right path of leaving the firearms and fighting with the ideology of *ahimsa*? Should I pick up guns again?"

Arnab was at a crossroads. There were examples on both sides of the equation. One said the path to freedom was assured, but the road was the toughest to travel. The Englishmen must be given the taste of their own medicine. A tooth for a tooth and an eye for an eye. The other said that without bloodshed, attaining freedom was a myth.

During those days, a notorious tribe of Kingla dacoits was active in the area. It worried Arnab as there was the possibility that they might loot the firearms which he was safeguarding. So Arnab decided to check his arsenal stock so that if they needed to fire some gunpowder, the guns were available. They were hidden in a place, the location of which was known only to him.

Situated around thirty miles away from Mussoorie was a temple of the Devalsari. Arnab had few loyalists with him in the struggle for freedom, but no one was close enough for him to take along to the secret temple of Shiva. Moreover, the road to Devalsari was challenging, as one had to walk most of the way. Thankfully, the tall deodar trees made the jungle dense, and it was easy to hide from the English.

The challenging task of the uphill walk and crossing the jungle without a hint of light would be deterrent to many, but Arnab was familiar with the terrain. The path had hidden landmarks along the way, which only he could recognize. A few piles of big rocks or a unique pattern of deodar trees were vital clues that he carefully discovered and marked. He was the only one who could recognize and remember them.

After half a day of a long, tiring walk, he finally reached the temple. He opened the door of the temple and prayed to Lord Shiva. He walked to the left corner of the entrance. There was a tiny door. He opened it and went down the stairs. It led to a dark room filled with damp air. He slowly walked to a big wooden box and opened it. It was full of English pistols and a few grenades.

Arnab looked at the firearms with wet eyes, hoping that one day he would witness India walking free from the shackles of the British. He had stood very close to crossing the thin line of fighting the war with firearms instead of uprooting the British with ahimsa. He closed the box.

Arnab had gone to Devalsari to test his firearms, but he returned without firing a single bullet. Probably, because he knew that one does not always need cartridges, but courage to attain freedom.

And he knew in his heart that he may never need the weapons again.

***

Arinjay could only think of one person who ticked all the criteria for keeping the Agha Netra safe. So he got up and walked towards Sylverton. When Arinjay reached there, he met a small group of Gandhians. They were raising their voices against the recent oppression of Britishers in Mussoorie.

Arinjay quietly sat between them and started to echo their voices.

"Britishers, go back! Long live India!"

Few British sepoys were watching them from a distance like an eagle watching prey. It was a peaceful protest, so the sepoys were waiting for them to make one mistake before they could swing their batons at them. The protestors knew that whatever happened, they were not to confront the sepoys.

Arinjay asked the group in a low voice about Arnab. None of them noticed Arinjay asking about Arnab. After a few unsuccessful attempts, Arinjay shouted,

"Has anyone of you seen Arnab?"

The sepoys did not like the shouting, and began walking towards the Gandhians. As the sepoys neared, the Gandhians started to run haphazardly. Arinjay got up hurryingly in that chaos, but suddenly someone pulled his hand. When Arinjay turned to see who it was, it was none other than Arnab.

He kept pulling Arinjay out of the Sylverton ground.

"What are you doing here?" Arnab asked, surprised.

"I was looking for you. And, today, I need help," Arinjay pleaded.

Arinjay showed him the Agha Netra.

"Promise me that you will keep this with you. You will never open it. And protect it till someone comes looking for it."

"What it is? What is inside it?" Arnab asked.

"Even I don't know the answer to that. But whatever it is, all I know that it is very powerful. That eye on the box is a curse. But only to them who will open it," Arinjay smirked.

"But who will come and when?" Arnab was baffled.

"A messenger will come. He may come today, tomorrow, after a week or a month. He might come when you are alive, or he may even come when your next few generations are old. But yes, he will come. One fine day, he certainly will."

Arnab was puzzled and overwhelmed. He replied as he looked at the box.

"You saved me that day. I owe you this. I will keep this with me, and if no one comes, my next generations will keep it with them till someone comes looking for it," Arnab said solemnly.

"What you are promising me is much more than what I have done for you," Arinjay said and handed the Agha Netra to Arnab.

"This evil eye will protect your family until you open the box. You protect this box, and this box will protect you. It's not a liability, Arnab; it's an asset. That day I protected you from the sergeant, and today, I am giving you something which will protect you for generations."

Arinjay patted Arnab's shoulder before he disappeared into the crowd.

***

Days, weeks, and months passed by. Arinjay had started his life in Xiamen. Poverty was still hanging around their necks like a snake. They tried their best, but apart from shelter and food provided by his uncle, he wasn't able to improve their situation in any manner.

One day, he saw his mother holding a few bundles of currency notes and a couple of gold coins. Arinjay was shocked to see so much money in her hand.

"From where did you get so much money?"

"My brother gave it to me."

"Your brother? But he's never given us a single penny since we've reached here," Arinjay said in surprise. Then suddenly something struck his mind. He held his mother by her arm and asked in a loud voice.

"Did you tell him about the Agha Netra?"

His mother looked at him in shock for a second, then started to laugh like a maniac.

"Yes, I sold the Agha Netra. I told them it is with you!" She laughed again.

Arinjay saw that his mother was in the grip of the devil. She was not herself.

"Today, you've lost your son. I told you, Ma, that my loyalty and love have the same price tag. It's invaluable. You took away my loyalty. I am taking away your love… your son from you. Goodbye, Mother."

Arinjay rushed out of the house with the Agha Netra's duplicate box. His mother helplessly watched him go. She knew he would never forgive her. She was rich, but she had lost her son.

Arinjay boarded a bus and asked for a ticket for the last stop. The person handed over the ticket. Arinjay asked the girl who was sitting beside him, showing her the ticket,

"Which place is this ticket for?"

She smiled.

"That is the last bus stop. Guangzhou."

Arinjay looked at the ticket, smiled, and put it back into his pocket.

Chapter 6

Am I Alisha?

Year 2022, somewhere in Mussoorie

The soft sun rays, soft and diffuse, coming through the half-open window were bouncing off Alisha's face. Her face was glowing as she snuggled into her blanket. The mellow winter sun of Mussoorie wasn't a hindrance to her sleep; instead, it was making her warm and cosy.

"Wake up, Alisha! It's already seven o'clock!"

Her mother burst into her room.

Alisha moved her head a little in an attempt to bury it inside the cushion. She knew it was a failed attempt to block her ears from the screeching voice.

"You will be late as usual. Get up, Alisha! Quickly."

Her mother shook her arms to wake her up.

Alisha opened one eye and looked at her mother.

"Do you believe in dreams that come true, Ma?" she asked her.

"I don't have much time to think about it. You get a better job and settle down, and only then I can say that dreams come true!" Alisha's mother sat beside her while running her fingers through her hair.

"I am not leaving this city, and I am not leaving you alone. You'll have to wait for your dreams to come true. Mussoorie must find a good job for me," Alisha said, slowly moving her head from the cushion and placing it on her mother's lap.

"You won't get a job here. How many times has your aunt called you to Delhi? Why don't you—"

"Not again, Ma!" Alisha cut her short.

"You never listen to me. And then you ask me whether dreams come true," Alisha's mother said worryingly.

"Look at this city. How can I leave Ma and Mussoorie behind?" Alisha sat on the bed, smiled, and continued.

"Now, before we start to argue, let me freshen up and see you at the breakfast table. I have to rush, as my students will be waiting for me." Alisha got down from her bed.

Alisha's father had died when she was in the final year of post graduation. That was four years back. After her father's death, she and her mother looked after each other. They were more than mother and daughter, rather bosom friends.

Now Alisha's mother wanted Alisha to go to Delhi and get a job. She wanted her to get settled. But she knew Alisha would never leave her alone in Mussoorie. However, deep in her heart, her mother was also not willing to send Alisha out of Mussoorie. What was bothering her greatly was that Alisha's condition was becoming more and more severe. She couldn't even remember faces anymore.

Alisha was in her late twenties. She was of medium-height, slim, with midnight black silky hair and a beautiful photogenic face. Her demure personality and soothing voice were proof of the introvert that she was.

After freshening up, Alisha sat down at the breakfast table while her mother was in the kitchen, making toast. She picked up a shining plate kept in front of her, looked at her clear reflection in it, and asked her mother in a stammering voice.

"Is that me, Ma?"

"Is she beautiful?" her mother asked her.

"Yeah, she is."

"Of course, then it is you. Who else will it be? Can there be anyone else be so beautiful in this world?" his mother smiled.

"Then why can't I recognize myself when I look so beautiful?" she stammered with a frown.

"Maybe because God doesn't want you to be proud about your beauty," her mother said softly.

Alisha smiled.

"When will I be able to recognize myself, Ma? When will I know that it's me?"

Her mother could sense her pain. She shouted from the kitchen.

"Don't keep staring at the plate now; pour some juice from the bottle. I will be there in a jiffy with the toast."

Alisha looked at the plate again and realized that the face had the smile missing. She was not able to recognize herself.

"Why did you ask me that whether dreams come true?" Her mother pulled up a chair beside Alisha and asked.

"I saw a dreadful dream early in the morning. And I pray that it does not come true; people say dreams which you see in the morning always come true," Alisha said worryingly.

"Not always. But you look worried, Alisha. Listen, just spell it out. This will help keep your mood light in the college, and you can focus on your work then," her mother insisted as she handed her the glass of juice.

Sipping the juice, Alisha leaned back and looked at her mother.

"I saw in my dream that I went to a garment shop to exchange the kurta that I had bought one day earlier. It was just one size bigger than what I wanted. So, I decided to exchange it for a smaller size. You told me that I should keep it, but I insisted. When I reached the shop, I met a security guard outside. He saw me and greeted me with a smile. I, too, smiled back, slightly bowed my head. His dress was dusty because he was standing on the road most of the time. However, there was a shiny object hanging on his chest; someone said he earned the medal in a war. That was the only thing shining brightly on his body. I walked inside the shop. As soon as I entered, I heard the screeching sound of the brakes of a car. I swiftly turned to see what had happened. In that split second... in the blink of an eye, a car crashed into the shop's signboard and ran over the security guard. I screamed and ran towards him. The last thing I remember was that there he was in a pool of blood, his medal completely drenched in it." Alisha paused, and after a few seconds, she said,

"And I woke up. I looked at the clock; it was early morning, around three a.m. I got up from my bed and drank a glass of water. I let out a sigh of relief that it was thankfully only a dreadful dream. After a while, I fell asleep again." Alisha went quiet.

"It's sad indeed. You've told me everything, now forget about it. It was a bad dream, and it happens with everyone. You will feel okay now."

Her mother held her hand.

"Now quickly go to college. Else, you will be late again."

"Yeah it's better I leave now," Alisha replied.

***

The college was not far from her house. The road to college was close to the Mall Road. While she passed by the market, her curiosity spiked when she saw the shop she had seen in her dream just on the other side of the Mall Road. She asked herself, *does that shop really exist?* Then it struck her that she was running late. She would come back later in the evening to search for the shop after college was over.

Around 9 a.m. she reached the MJK, Maharani Janki Kumari college. She parked the scooter and went to the staff room to mark her attendance. She entered the staff room and saw a dwarfish guy in his early fifties sitting on a chair. Alisha scanned him.

"Good morning, Sanjay sir."

This guy looked at Alisha and shook his head in disappointment.

"It has been two years since you joined the college, Alisha. We meet every day in the staff room, but still you can't remember my name," the guy said.

"Oh, I am sorry, Ram sir. I just forgot," she said apologetically.

"Mehta! My name is Ranjit Mehta," he said, frustrated, and walked out of the staff room.

Alisha was perplexed.

"Ranjit Mehta, okay, Ranjit Mehta. How did I miss the short hair and red pen in his pocket? It was enough for me to remember he is Ranjit..." she murmured and came out of the staff room.

The best way to remember the faces was to spot a sign. So instead of remembering someone's face, she recalled an object, mark, or something that always remained with the person. In the case of Ranjit Mehta, she remembered him as a person with the red fountain pen in his pocket and short hair.

Alisha's connecting with people was not going well, and she felt she was not socially acceptable. Imagine constantly meeting people who recognize you, yet you struggle to remember them in return. She always knew that difficulty in facial recognition led to frustration and embarrassment, like in the case of Ranjit Mehta. What was more worrying was the social anxiety that followed these encounters.

Ranjit Mehta was not the only case in the college. For her the bigger worry was remembering faces of students in the lab. How many indicators to remember so many faces? She did her best to devise many tricks but none of them worked, and she failed to connect with the students.

Alisha was missing out on a fundamental aspect of human interaction. Every face she met was a stranger to her. Recognizing a friend in a crowd or remembering a colleague's face became complex and stressful tasks. Things became worse when she looked at herself in the mirror.

This led to a sense of alienation or disconnectedness from others, and she avoided social situations to prevent the discomfort of being unable to recognize people. She felt insecure about appearing rude or indifferent when failing to recognize acquaintances or even close friends and family. Over time, this eroded her self-confidence and contributed to a sense of isolation.

Since her childhood, Alisha has been a shy girl, and being face blind developed a loneliness in her.

While coming back from college she made an attempt to spot the shop, but she was unable to locate it. Finally giving up the search she rode back home.

Whenever Alisha's mother saw Alisha being worried about something, she'd encourage her to talk about it. But Alisha as she grew up, would keep her worries to herself, rather than make her mother worry. She learnt to hide things that were bothering her rather than sharing them.

The dream was working as a catalyst with her face blindness for her worries.

Thinking all about the dream, Alisha walked into her house and saw a girl sitting on the sofa. She looked at her and wondered who she was. The girl was reading a magazine, and she didn't know Alisha was looking at her. Wondering who the girl was, Alisha she quietly stepped towards her room.

"Wait!" The girl looked at Alisha.

Alisha stopped.

"I had a haircut and thought of showing you how I look," the girl smiled. Seeing Alisha's confused face, she added, "Sana, remember me? Sana?"

It was her best friend Sana.

Alisha said happily, "Sana! Gosh! You look so stunning that I can't believe it is you. I left wondering who this beautiful girl is and what she is doing in my house."

"No, no. I know you didn't recognize me," Sana giggled.

Hearing the laughter, Alisha mother came outside and said, "Sana! Now, I know why you were desperately waiting for Alisha. So that you can make fun of her, haan?" she chuckled.

"No, Aunty, it's not like that. I have another reason." Sana pulled out a packet from her bag and handed it over to Alisha.

"I bought this for you. Now quickly try it out. If this doesn't fit, we can exchange it."

Sana has bought a kurta for Alisha. She always shopped for Alisha. Their choice of clothes and colours were similar.

Alisha went inside to try on the kurta. It almost fit, and she liked it. When her mother saw it, she said,

"It would be a perfect fit if it was a size smaller."

"Okay, we will exchange it tomorrow," Sana said.

"No, I think it's okay. You should keep it; there is no harm in wearing one size bigger," Alisha's mother said.

But Alisha insisted on exchanging it for a smaller one.

After Sana left, Alisha looked at her mother.

"Ma, it seems like it's coming true."

"What?" her mother asked.

"My dream." She took a deep breath.

"It is the same kurta that I saw in my dream," Alisha said in a trembling voice and walked into her room.

Chapter 7

The Court and the Mystery

The MJK college was fighting a legal dispute on land that was purchased by the college trust. A barren land adjacent to the college was acquired to build a new sports facility that the administration had wanted for a long time. The college had appointed a young lawyer, Rajat Roy, to handle the case.

The board members were sitting around a table that was shaped like a horseshoe. Rajat swiftly knocked on the door, briskly walked in and sat at one end of it.

"Apologies for keeping you waiting. But trust me, this time, our argument in the case is much stronger. The court can't keep our work on hold. The dispute is between two brothers on the sale amount."

Rajat attempted to be convincing and was confident when he spoke, glancing at every board member. Rajat conveyed his honest opinion and convinced the board about his capability to win the case.

Though the board was happy to bring Rajat to fight the case, at the same time, a few frowns in the room questioned his capability to win it.

After a few minutes of the closing remarks, the board meeting was dismissed.

Rajat came out of the board meeting and decided to grab some food in the college canteen. There he saw a girl coming out of the lab. She looked confused and tired. The expression on her face was so unique and beautiful that Rajat kept looking at her. At that moment, Alisha saw Rajat staring at her. She squinted and walked away swiftly from there.

"Excuse me!" Rajat shouted.

Alisha stopped and looked at him.

"Do you know the way to the canteen?" he asked her.

"Go straight, take the first left and then right from that door. It's near the scooter parking area," she said and walked out of the alley.

Rajat thanked her. He reached the canteen and called his assistant.

"Shivpal has filed the affidavit. Please can you get me all the details of what is in it? Looks like it will take some time to gain the trust of the board members of MJK."

***

Alisha went with Sana to the shop to exchange the kurta. As they reached close to the shop, Alisha looked worried and began breathing heavily. Sana looked at her.

"What happened? We are only going to exchange a kurta, not going to a war. So, calm down," she giggled.

Alisha nodded. As soon as they got down from the autorickshaw, Alisha searched for the security guard she had seen in her dream. The biggest worry was that she wouldn't remember his face, and to fuel her anxiety, no security guard was present near the shop. For a moment, she was relieved.

Her heartbeat slowly came down to normal, and she walked towards the shop. As they were walking into the shop, a voice called out.

"Madam, your money."

Alisha turned and saw a security guard standing behind her, holding a hundred-rupee note. She noticed his dusty clothes, but the medal was missing from his chest. She let out a sigh of relief. Then while she was looking at him, one guy came to the guard and asked him about something in his pocket. Alisha turned to go into the shop, and the guard took out a medal from his pocket. Alisha noticed something shiny, so she turned again to look at the guard.

Except for his face, she could now exactly match everything she had seen in the dream. Her heartbeat spiked again as she broke out in a cold sweat. Unaware of Alisha's condition, Sana pulled Alisha's hand to bring her into the shop, but Alisha kept looking at the guard. Suddenly, a loud screeching was heard; Alisha closed her eyes and shouted, *"No!"*

A loud bang was heard; she turned and saw a car had crashed into the shop's signboard, and the guard had been run over. It was the moment the unfortunate dream came true.

She ran towards the body of the security guard, screaming and crying. Sana ran behind Alisha and tried to soothe her. Sana was appalled to see Alisha's reaction; it was as if someone close to her was involved. Alisha reached the blood-drenched body of the security guard. She saw the medal and fainted.

Sana shouted for help in that chaos. A tall man rushed to the scene, picked Alisha, and rushed towards the nearby hospital, as an ambulance arrived for the guard.

Alisha felt someone sprinkling water on her face. She woke up. She saw a girl standing beside her and a man standing near her leg. Alisha looked at the girl again closely. There was a mole just below her nose, and she had her hair in a ponytail that seemed familiar.

"Sana?" Alisha asked, squinting her eyes.

"Gosh, you are back. Yeah, Alisha, obviously it's me. What happened to you?" Sana went close to her and held her hand.

Then Alisha looked at the guy.

"I am sorry. Do I know you? Who are you?" she asked.

"No, you don't know me. But we met in the college. Briefly! Remember, I asked you about the way to the canteen?" Rajat said.

"Rajat helped me to bring you to the hospital, Alisha. He was there when you fainted," Sana explained.

"Thanks, Rajat."

It was difficult for Alisha to remember Sana's face, so remembering

Rajat's was impossible. For Rajat, it hardly mattered as he knew they had met momentarily in college.

Alisha came back home with Sana. Her unfortunate dream turned out to be true. It was a shock for her. The pain of not remembering the face of the security guard was more hurting. She could have looked for him beforehand and saved his life, but at the same time, it's less painful when you cannot remember the face of the person who died. It would help her forget, though she'd always remember the horrific incident.

That night, Alisha slept and woke up with a start at 3 a.m. It was another dream. Another dreadful one.

***

The next day at the breakfast table, Alisha was quiet. Her mother knew Alisha still needed some time to recover from the ordeal. She sat beside Alisha and gently tapped her shoulder.

"You have to forget that incident, Alisha. There is nothing you could have done," her mother consoled Alisha.

"I could have done a lot, Ma, I could have saved him. I was standing there, and he spoke to me. It is just because I have this condition that I am helpless."

Alisha miserably smiled and continued, "You know what, last night I saw another dream, Ma. This time I saw a girl falling from a building."

Alisha paused for a second.

"I can't take it anymore, Ma; why this is happening to me? Why not someone else." Alisha's eyes were wet, and a tear rolled down her face. She was in pain and felt helpless.

"No, No. Alisha, not every dream will come true. It won't happen again," her mother pacified her.

"It will happen again, Ma; it will happen again. I know that." Alisha sobbed and left the breakfast table without a bite.

Alisha's mother knew it would be hard for Alisha to move past the horrific incident. But the worrying part was the dreams. Alisha was now able to see the future of someone who was going to die.

***

Rajat was sitting in the canteen of MJK college and going through his files. He sipped on a cup of hot tea. While he was thinking about the case, he saw the canteen boy fiddling with a Rubik's cube. Rajat waved his hand in a gesture to tell the boy to bring tea. When the boy came, Rajat asked him curiously,

"You like the Rubik's cube? You know how to solve it?"

"No, I don't. But one day, I will," he replied.

"That's good. Are you new here? What's your name?" Rajat asked.

"I am Arvind. People call me Aru," he paused and replied, "and sometimes they call me Shortcut," Aru added shaking his head sadly.

"Don't worry, Aru. One day you will overcome all the problems in your life, including this Rubik's cube," he said trying to cheer him up.

Aru went back to the counter, and Rajat started to read the files. From one perspective, the case was not strong enough for the college to start work on the ground. It's just that the court had put a stay because Rampal was creating more nuisance than his brother Shivpal, and also had the support of local people. Rajat had dealt with a few cases before, but this one was unique. Now, the primary goal of Rajat was for MJK to somehow get the hold of the ground to start the work. Thinking about his case. Rajat began to walk towards the staff room. While he was walking across the long passage which connects the staff room to the canteen, he saw Alisha coming out of the lab.

He swiftly went to her.

"How are you feeling now?" he asked concerned.

Alisha gave him a strange look. This time Rajat was baffled.

"You remember me? I am the same guy who took you to the hospital after you fainted in that shop—"

Before Rajat could finish what he was saying, Alisha had crossed the passage and gone out. Rajat couldn't believe that Alisha couldn't remember him. This time, he was disappointed as well as hurt.

Rajat went to his desk in the staff room and pondered to understand what Rampal wanted from this move. If the land was in dispute, it would make its value far less than the market price unless someone was paying him more than what he got from MJK for that land. Or was there something else?

While he was leaning on his chair and thinking about all this, he heard Alisha's voice in the staff room. He saw Alisha was talking to someone. She looked sad. Rajat knew the reason behind her sadness, but he couldn't be sure.

A voice behind him said,

"It has been more than two years since the staff meet in the staff room every day, but she hardly remembers anyone. Wonder why is she so arrogant. Why does she ignore her own colleagues?"

"But why does she do that?"

"Might be because she is beautiful, and we pay the premium of not being remembered by her," the guys grinned and walked out of the staff room.

Rajat now had an answer to why Alisha was behaving so strangely.

Chapter 8

Face... What?

Alisha was yet to come out of the first trauma, when the second one came knocking at her door. She was worried about this becoming the new normal in her life. The only one she could think of other than her mother to speak to was Sana. She called Sana up and asked her to meet her in the college.

"So, tell me what happened," Sana asked as they sat down at a table in the canteen.

"I am not sure how I should tell you. But nowadays, something happening to me which is not normal," Alisha said with her lips quivering.

Sana looked at her with concern.

"Well, I knew something was amiss when you screamed and ran towards that guard. I was appalled to see your reaction. Tell me, honestly, do you know him?" Sana asked her.

"Yes and no," Alisha paused and said "It's complicated."

"Yes indeed. I have known you for ages now. But I have never seen you reacting like this. What exactly went wrong that day?" Sana's curiosity was piqued.

"I saw that scene unfolding in my dreams the previous night," Alisha whispered.

"What?" Sana was surprised.

Alisha told all about her dream. After listening to what Alisha told her, there was complete silence. A sudden voice broke the silence in like a hammer hitting a rock.

"Hey Sana!"

It was Rajat.

"What are you doing here, Rajat? Nice to see you again," Sana said.

"I am at MJK for my work. So how is your friend feeling now," Rajat frowned.

"You can ask her; she is all ears," Sana smiled.

"Are you sure? I tried asking her, but she didn't bother to respond. So, I am not trying my luck second time," Rajat smirked. "You know that self-respect and all. I am picky about it," he added.

Sana looked at Alisha and then at Rajat asked, "What's going on?"

Sana told Alisha that Rajat was the same guy who had taken her to the hospital when she fainted a few days ago.

Alisha was puzzled, confused and feeling bad that she didn't recognize Rajat. She got up from her chair.

"I am sorry, Rajat. There is a lot that is happening around me and I am too weak to handle all this. The only thing I can say right now is that I am sorry."

Alisha turned and walked out of the canteen.

"Has she always been like that, or has something changed after the incident?" Rajat asked Sana.

"I've known her since we were kids. Alisha is shy and an introvert. The last thing she will do is hurt anyone," Sana told Rajat before running after Alisha.

Rajat watched their retreating backs. Battling in his mind were two thoughts: that what Alisha was doing was not usual, and second, Sana was portraying Alisha as an ordinary girl, which she was not. Rajat didn't expect to win accolades or be welcomed by Alisha like a hero or saviour. What he did that day was what anyone would have done for her, but Alisha's strange behaviour was something he could not accept. He decided that he would figure out why Alisha was so weird someday. And that day would come soon.

***

Rajat reached the court with his mind blustering with an endless stream of thoughts about Shivpal and the affidavit. Finally, the court session began. In the first instance the lawyer of Shivpal pulled out the affidavit and presented it to the judge.

The judge took the affidavit and asked,

"What is this, Mr Jagdeesh? "

"My client wants to withdraw from the deal. As per agreement clause number 16, if my client presents a reason and if both parties agree, he has the right to withdraw."

"The land is already sold, and Shivpal has signed on the agreement. Now, what is this affidavit about?" the judge said looking at the document and read one line which surprised him.

And in my dream, he came and asked me not to sell the land.

Rajat frowned as he was expecting that affidavits had something to do with the sale price of the land. With that baffled mind, he raised an objection that he was not notified about the new affidavit, and he wanted to take time to read what was in it.

The judge was worried and puzzled after reading the document. He looked at Rajat.

"You must look at it. I think the basis of withdrawing from the agreement is too weak. This affidavit is strange."

The court session was concluded for the day, and a new date was decided on after two weeks. Rajat asked for a date sooner which the judge denied saying,

"I don't think this case will be over so soon, Mr Rajat. Take your time to read the affidavit."

Rajat nodded his head and walked out of the courtroom. Shivpal swiftly followed Rajat, and just outside the courtroom, he whispered in his ears.

"He is watching. Save yourself from the eye."

Rajat looked at Shivpal. His eyes were bloodshot, widened and slightly wet. It was apparent that he was worried and angry.

Shivpal's face didn't convey that he had greed for money. Those words had a cryptic rather than a straightforward meaning. Rajat got the copy of the affidavit and drove back to college. What had happened in court in those few minutes? The judge was baffled after reading the affidavit, and Shivpal's cryptic message was something Rajat did not anticipate. He reached the MJK canteen and sat there thinking about it.

He looked at Aru and asked him to bring a cup of tea. Just next to his table, he saw Alisha worried, lost in her own thoughts. Rajat thought he had been too rude to her in the parking area and decided to apologize.

He dragged his chair and sat beside Alisha's table.

"Look, Alisha, I am sorry. I was rude this morning. It was unusual of me to behave that way."

Alisha could now remember the voice. She knew him. She looked at him.

"See, I know this seems odd, but would you mind telling me who you are? I know that I know you, but I can't recall your name."

"I am Rajat!"

"Yes! Thanks for reminding me, Rajat." Alisha smiled. "It's fine about what happened in the morning. These things are the new normal in my life."

"New normal? You probably don't want to hear this, but I will say it, anyway. Why are you so arrogant that you don't even bother to remember anyone?" Rajat asked.

"Arrogance?" Alisha smirked and sighed. "I am not arrogant, Rajat, I am face blind!"

Rajat looked at her in surprise, "Face what?"

"Face blind or Prosopagnosia. It's a medical condition where I may know a name but I just can't put a face to it. I don't remember faces, Rajat," Alisha explained.

Chapter 9

The Triangle

'Face blind.'

Rajat had never heard of that term before. This word defined and clarified all doubts about why Alisha behaved in such a strange manner with him and the others in college all these years. But at the same time, it was not easy for Rajat to digest that face blindness could be the sole reason. The lawyer's mind thought of putting this condition through a litmus test.

The college organized a board meeting two days after the court hearing to decide the next move. All bets were placed on Rajat to win the case. But the affidavit was about to put up a new challenge no one had ever dreamt of.

Rajat decided that in following two days he would go through the content in the affidavit and put up a convincing argument to the college board that would boost their confidence in him. At least up a few notches.

In a very short period, Alisha had met Rajat quite a few times. In that short span, she had developed a unique feeling towards Rajat. She had never been with any other boy. And Rajat was the only one with whom Alisha had talked about her face blindness.

"You told him? Are you serious?" Sana asked surprisingly when they met later at a cafe.

"Yeah, I did. I don't know how it happened. I just said it even though it's a very personal thing that only you and Ma had known. But now, Rajat does too," Alisha said with a puzzled face.

"Hello, Alisha. The very next day, he will walk right past you, and you will never even recognize him. If he decides to forget you, then the story will end there. How can you trust him so much?" Sana could not grasp the fact that Alisha revealed her condition to someone she barely knew.

"I don't know what's happening, Sana. It's better I should forget that I met him," Alisha said and shrugged her shoulders.

"To forget anyone, you need to fulfil a fundamental condition. That is to remember them. Lucky that I always make a ponytail, and I have this black mole on my face so that you can recognize me," Sana said shaking her head.

Alisha wasn't paying attention to what Sana was telling her. Instead, she was slowly transported to a different place. This place was calm and lovely. She kept asking herself what was happening to her, but there was no answer to the quietness. Whatever it was, it was a cozy and mushy feeling which Alisha didn't want to let go of.

Alisha knew that Rajat usually sat in the college canteen mostly in the afternoon, reading. So the next day she went to the canteen in the afternoon and waited for Rajat. She was expecting that as she had told Rajat about her condition, Rajat would recognize her instead of her recognizing Rajat. It was strange waiting for someone, hoping that another person would recognize you. Even after an hour, no one came up to her. Alisha remembered what Sana said. *He will walk right past you, and you will never even recognize him. If he decides to forget you, the story will end there.*

It was a depressing afternoon for Alisha. She knew that Rajat wouldn't do that to her. In the last few days he was the one who had come and to meet Alisha. After a long wait in the canteen, Alisha left the and started to walk towards the parking area. Rajat was walking towards the canteen from the same walkway and saw Alisha coming down. That litmus test struck him like lightning. He swiftly went in front of her.

"Hi."

Alisha looked at him in a familiar manner. Rajat looked at her reaction and it felt as though she knew who he was. But at that very moment, she asked, "Do I know you?"

Rajat said to himself, *Now, she might be making that up.*

So he replied, "No, we haven't met. Please can you tell me the way to the staffroom?"

Alisha pointed her finger in the direction of the staffroom and left. That reaction and response didn't convince Rajat that she was face blind as she claimed to be.

Rajat stood there looking at Alisha, walking away. He then rolled the paper in his hand and walked towards the canteen. Alisha after walking a few steps turned back to look at the guy, asking herself,

Is he Rajat? And then she replied to herself, *No, Rajat will not do that to me.*

In the canteen, Rajat ordered a cup of tea and his phone buzzed. It was his college friend Kevin.

"I got to know that you are in Mussoorie. You are in heaven, my friend. Guess what? I will be in town tomorrow. So, tell me where we should meet?" Kevin asked cheerily.

"I am at this college – MJK," Rajat continued, "Meeting you will be a treat, my buddy. Come down to MJK; I have made it my home nowadays. Also, there is an interesting case which I am handling. I promise that it will give you the kicks." Rajat chuckled.

"No. No case. I am in Mussoorie to relax for a couple of days only. So big 'no' to work," Kevin said.

"Okay, got it, pal. Come down, let me show you around then," Rajat chuckled.

"That's like my friend. I will give you a call when I reach the college."

Rajat hung up and smiled, looking at the phone. Kevin's phone call refreshed Rajat's college memories.

He started to go through the affidavit from the start. It was written in the simplest of language, and anyone could easily understand why

Shivpal wanted to pull out from the deal. But some words were baffling. One paragraph was most cryptic:

The land is the shape of a triangle. And it was with us since our great grandfather got the land from the king who was cursed by that evil eye. I have seen the eye's image in one of the paintings in the king's palace, just outside the city. The eye is red, and dark blue rays come out from the eyelids. As if they want to spread everywhere, but a triangle fences the eye's image. This triangle stops the rays to curse everyone on the planet. That eye and the blue rays will harm everyone, whoever comes in its path. And one day, he came in my dream. He came and asked me not to sell the land to anyone. Else, there will be a holocaust, and the blue curse will befall on each one of us."

Further, in the affidavit, Shivpal begged MJK college and Rampal to withdraw from the agreement, citing the reason that many lives were at stake. At first glance, it clearly felt like Shivpal was making up the story to get out of the agreement and sell this land to someone else for a considerable amount. But before Rajat could conclude anything, he wanted to go deeper into it and understand the truth. He met Rampal and also the others who knew Shivpal and the land. If Rajat would put up this story in front of the MJK management, they would clearly brush it aside, saying it was made up. And, also, they'd certainly judge Rajat as an individual influenced by fascinating mythical stories of the evil eye, and hence incapable of handling this case.

***

There was a sense of insecurity affecting Alisha. What if Rajat revealed her secret to the staff in the college? What if the management found it to be a reason to ask Alisha to leave the college? What would happen to her and her mother? It was essential for her to meet him and to tell Rajat to keep the secret to himself.

That night Alisha woke up again. She had the same dream of a girl falling off. She saw the clock. It was three in the morning. She was pained, wondering why she had seen the dream again. And above all, she couldn't do anything about it due to her condition.

The following day, Alisha told her mother about the dream. However, her mother again convinced Alisha that a dream does not always come true.

"It pains me, Ma when I can't do anything about it. I can't remember the faces; I can't help that girl. And one day, it will happen in front of me. I know I will be there watching it taking place." Alisha looked at her mother with her eyes wet. Again, this was a failed attempt by her mother to convince Alisha that what had happened in the past was just a coincidence, and it wouldn't happen again. Her pain was not about the dream, but the death about which she could not do anything.

***

Kevin reached MJK and called up Rajat. They were meeting after a couple of years.

"So, this college is keeping you away from beauty of Mussoorie. What is so special about the case?" Kevin smiled.

"It looked seemed to be an easy one earlier, but something happened yesterday."

Rajat paused, and after a deep breath he said,

"However as promised, I will not let you get involved in it. Enjoy the winter and let me treat you to MKJ's special tea." Rajat put his arm around Kevin's shoulder and ushered him towards the canteen. In the lobby Rajat saw Alisha going inside the lab. Alisha saw Rajat briefly, smiled and then went inside the lab room.

Rajat could figure out Alisha smiled at him as a stranger. But Rajat was not ready to accept her condition at face value. Then suddenly he looked at Kevin.

"I need your help," he said. "Don't say no. I will explain everything at the canteen," he smiled and jogged ahead with him.

They both reached the canteen and heard students talking about AI. Rajat called Aru.

"Hey Aru, please bring two cups of tea. And, what's going on? What is this AI?"

Aru smiled.

"Actually, I don't know. But these guys have been talking about it since morning."

"Must be something interesting. And what about your Rubik's cube? Did you solve it?"

Aru looked around, stretched, rolled his lips, pulled out the solved cube from his pocket, "Yes!"

"Well done! You look different today. Keep smiling," Rajat chuckled and asked him to bring two cups. Kevin was getting curious to know what Rajat wanted from him.

"So, here is the thing. You have to disguise yourself as me in front of someone. Don't worry; she will not recognize you if what she claims is true." Rajat folded his hands and leaned forward on the table.

"What? Who is she? Did you meet her before? In person? Or did you only chat on WhatsApp or on-call?" asked a baffled Kevin.

"I don't want to tell you anything more about it. Just pretend to be me and tell me how it goes. Don't worry; I won't put you in deep water. Trust me." Rajat smiled.

"But this is not ethical, Rajat. Tell me you are not cheating on someone."

"Do you think I can cheat on someone?" Rajat looked at Kevin.

"No."

"Then that's it. I will guide you, so don't worry," Rajat said.

"But why are you doing all this? And who is she?"

"It is a litmus test. And she is in this college. So just be confident in front of her."

Rajat looked at Kevin extended his hand. "Are you in, my friend?"

Kevin looked at Rajat. He shook his head and extended his hand.

"If something goes wrong, you know I am a lawyer, too. And you don't want me to stand prosecuting you in court," Kevin winked.

"Let me tell you that I know this before I asked for your help. So, I won't pick a fight with you, Kevin." Rajat laughed.

Rajat told Kevin that he wanted Kevin to meet Alisha as Rajat. He said to him that Alisha knew him. Rajat said he would watch them from afar.

Kevin agreed to it on one condition, if something went wrong, he had the right to let Alisha know the truth. Rajat agreed happily. Rajat's confidence that his plan would work also came from the fact that Kevin had a similar face cut which was enough to confuse Alisha.

Alisha wanted to meet Rajat and get a promise from him that he would keep her secret. She was anxious and worried. In that state of mind, she went to the canteen again, expecting Rajat to come up and meet her if he was around. While Rajat and Kevin were getting up from the table, Rajat saw Alisha. He nudged his friend.

"Are you ready, Kevin? There she is. I will sit near that table, and you go walk up to her. Pretend that you guys have met before. Remember you are Rajat."

"Why did I come to Mussoorie? And why did I meet you?" he shook his head in disappointment and went towards Alisha. Rajat followed Kevin and sat two tables away.

Kevin reached Alisha, held the chair in front, leaned forward and said,

"How are you doing today, Alisha?"

Alisha looked at him. She frowned.

"I am good. May I know who you are?"

Kevin trembled in nervousness. He looked at Rajat, who gave him a thumbs up.

Kevin stammered, "I am Rajat. Remember?"

Alisha looked at him.

"Rajat?" She paused, then suddenly she said, "Hey, where were you? I came here just to meet you. You know, Rajat, I have to discuss something extremely important."

Kevin was nervous, and he looked at Rajat again. Rajat was surprised that Alisha didn't recognize him. Rajat was partially convinced that what Alisha said about her condition was true. But he didn't want to end Kevin's pretence there, so he decided to sit and watch what would happen.

"You know what, Rajat. I know it's you, but I can't feel the same way as I did when I had met you earlier. There is something which is missing," Alisha said worryingly.

"Anyway, can we meet somewhere outside? How about Gully's Cafe near Mall Road? After college at five?" Alisha added and leaned forward to convince Kevin.

Kevin's heartbeat spiked; there was a sudden stab of fear. He was numb and felt an ache in the belly telling him not to say yes. His eyes darted at Alisha, and he slowly nodded his head.

Alisha was happy that she had finally found Rajat and that he had agreed to meet her at Gully's.

She got up and Kevin watched her go. Rajat was watching the scene all the while. As soon as Alisha left the canteen, Rajat guffawed.

"You almost got me killed. Whew, those were few minutes of horror that I survived." Kevin wiped the sweat on his forehead and said, "I am not going to Gully's; no way!"

Rajat controlled his laughter.

"What happened? Look at yourself; you look pale. She was not a monster. You behaved as if you were fearing for your life. Okay, I am sorry! But how can you break a promise? Especially when you promised a girl. Go man, have a coffee. See what she wants to tell you. And frankly, I am curious too and am wondering why she's called you to Gully's. She could have told you whatever she wanted to say here. Anyway, remember now you have a date at five. Be on time. I will meet you at your hotel."

Rajat convinced Kevin to meet her, and then return to the hotel later and tell him what had transpired, as he had to go and meet Rampal about the affidavit. Convincing Kevin was not that easy, and Kevin wondered why Rajat was doing this. However, he trusted his friend and agreed to meet Alisha.

Alisha felt a sense of relief that she'd meet Rajat. She WhatsApped Sana and told her that Rajat promised to meet her at Gully's. Sana was curious why she didn't tell Rajat at the canteen itself, instead of meeting outside.

***

Sana called Alisha.

"You should have told him at the college itself. Why do you want to drag it?"

Alisha said, "I didn't want to talk about it in college with students and staff around us, so I thought we'd meet outside."

"Whatever it is Alisha, I don't have a good feeling about it. It's not that Rajat is not a good guy, but don't trust anyone so soon. And remember, no one ever makes a mistake twice. If you make a mistake the second time, it's not a mistake but your choice," Sana continued.

"Anyway, I am going back to my desk. Mussoorie is full of tourists now. It is difficult for me to leave the reception at the hotel," Sana chuckled.

"Yeah, Golden Gate Hotel owes you a lot," Alisha giggled.

Sana hung up and went back to the reception of the Golden Gate Hotel. She had got this job a couple of months back. It was a job to fund her higher studies. She was very hopeful that one day she would reach the US and settle there after her studies.

Sana was a chatterbox. People say she got this job because of her extroverted nature and talkative personality. She had a lot of friends to hang around with, but she kept only a few very close to her heart. While working at the hotel reception, Sana had philosophical thoughts about the people around her. She felt that people always had some purpose when they check in into your life. Once the purpose is over, they may check out anytime. Some pay the bills, and some do not. But some stay for long. She weighed people by the first impression they created on her. Rajat had a helpful nature, but she knew he was a lawyer. And if you tell lawyers any secret, they will make the best use of it.

Sana reached her desk, and there were a couple of customers waiting. She stood behind the desk and smiled at the guy in front of her.

"How are you doing today? How may I help you, sir?"

"I hooked the tag to get my room cleaned, but it wasn't done," he said.

"I'm sorry about that, Sir. I'll check that for you right away. May I have your room number, please?" Sana asked.

"It is 1301"

"You are Kevin Shah?" Sana smiled.

"Yeah, I am Kevin."

"I will ask someone to follow you to your room, Sir. They will clean it right away. Anything else I can help you with?"

Kevin shook his head and said, "No."

Then instantly he turned back to Sana.

"May I ask how far is Gully's Cafe from here?"

"It's at the Mall Road, sir. If you take a cab, you will get there in ten minutes. But you will have to walk as the road will be closed for vehicles after five," Sana said.

"Thanks," Kevin looked at the name badge and added, "Thanks, Sana, for the information." And proceeded to walk towards the elevator.

Kevin was not in the mood to meet Alisha. He knew what he was doing was not right. But the confusion was why Rajat wanted him to meet Alisha. Rajat and Kevin had been good friends in college. One thing which Kevin liked about Rajat was his devotion to any subject.

Rajat always held the problem with claw and teeth till he solved it. All his dedication and passion towards any issue made him a fighter. But he ever never cheated anyone; he never told a lie nor did he impersonate someone. So, what was happening this time?

Kevin's head was teeming with these thoughts as he reached his room.

"Excuse me, sir," a voice called out.

Kevin looked around and saw Sana standing behind him.

"Hey, what happened?"

"Sir, you forgot your room keys. "

"Oh! how can I do that? It seems like the coffee date at Gully's is making me nervous," Kevin smiled.

"A date? Don't worry, sir, whoever she is, you will win her over. Best of luck, sir," Sana said and walked towards the elevator.

Kevin knew that calling his meeting with Alisha a date was undoubtedly the wrong choice of words. Deep in his heart, he was not happy impersonating Rajat. Kevin always lent a helping hand to his friends, but he had never been a masquerade. One thing was sure, that if Alisha came to know the truth, he would not hesitate to come clean.

He reached Gully's and sat waiting for Alisha. The cafe was located in a busy area and had a few offices around. This place was always teeming with office goers in the evening. While looking around, he saw Alisha standing at the stairs leading to the door and peeping inside. Kevin was surprised. He went to Alisha and tapped her on her shoulder. Alisha turned and saw a man behind her. She gave a surprised look and squinted her eyes. Kevin was shocked at her reaction. They had just met a few hours back.

He said in a stammering voice, "Hello Alisha, it's me."

He looked at Alisha expecting that she'd remember him. After a few seconds he said, "It's Rajat."

"Oh sorry, Rajat."

She smiled and continued, "Now you know how depressing and frustrating my condition is."

Alisha's condition made her lonely and kept her socially at bay most of the time. Telling Rajat about her condition was the last thing she wanted to do. It was certainly difficult to speak about it freely, but there was no other choice.

Kevin was baffled and wondered what condition she was talking about.

"Rajat, I could have told you in the college canteen but you know there were students and staff who might hear our conversation." She paused, looked around and said, "I want you to keep my face blindness as secret. If you talk about it in the college, the MJK staff may not like it and it may even lead to me losing my job."

Alisha was worried. She looked at Kevin with folded hands and soulful eyes.

Kevin didn't know what to say. He didn't know what Alisha was talking about. In that perplexed moment he smiled and nodded his head. That slight nod gave Alisha the comfort she was looking for. She smiled in relief. They sat at the coffee table for a while and chatted. During the whole conversation Kevin never talked about the MJK court case. Alisha was a little surprised at that. She thought that probably Rajat wanted to keep the coffee table conversation personal.

After a while they left Gully's and started to walk towards the place where Alisha had parked the scooter. Kevin and Alisha were mostly quiet. Kevin wanted to go back to the hotel quickly but Alisha was taking small steps so that they could amble in the lanes. She never went out for coffee with anyone other than Sana. Walking along the lanes with Rajat felt special, and she didn't want the evening to end soon.

"I have never seen you so quiet before. Is something bothering you?" Alisha asked without looking at Kevin.

"No, it's just... I am busy with my thoughts... about other things," Kevin stammered.

"I know it's about the court case you are working on. But I am sure you will find a way out," Alisha replied.

"I want to be free... and yes, I hope the case ends very soon," Kevin replied.

"You don't like being here? Mussoorie? MJK?"

Kevin looked at Alisha and replied,

"I pray that I don't start liking this place. Else, it will be hard for me to leave Mussoorie."

Alisha could make out that Rajat was feeling low. She wondered whether it was her company that he wasn't enjoying or the MJK court case which was stressing him a lot.

When they reached Alisha's scooter, two guys around six feet tall, wearing baseball caps and skin-fit black t-shirts, rolled up to their muscular arms, came towards Kevin. They held his hand and pulled him to the corner of the wall. Alisha watched helplessly, in shock. One man held Kevin's collar and said something that Alisha could not hear. Kevin resisted in anger, and then the man twisted and held his arm. To that reaction, the second one punched Kevin in the stomach and then on his forehead. Kevin's forehead struck the wall, and there was a trickle of blood. Alisha shouted at them. They looked up at her and left the place calmly.

"Are you okay? Who are they?" Alisha rushed to Kevin.

Kevin calmed her and told her that he was getting threats because of the MJK case.

"I am okay," he said though he was shaken.

After seeing Alisha off, Kevin took a taxi and returned to the hotel.

Chapter 10

Curious Eyes

Rajat left for the palace to see the picture of the evil eye. The affidavit didn't have a clear meaning; it had a message and Rajat had to read between the lines. There were two schools of thought swirling in his mind. One was to raise an objection on the affidavit and quash it on the grounds of it being mythological and make it irrelevant. Or look closely at the claim made by Shivpal so that it could be challenged and prove it wrong with solid evidence. And the best bet would be to prove that there was no such evil eye at all. After an hour-long bike ride, he reached the palace.

It was an old building. The facade had lost its glory a few hundred years back. Apart from the archaeological signboard placed just outside the gate, there was nothing new in that building. It seemed like the government did not have the budget to look after the palace. The palace was open for people without any entry tickets. Still, there were no visitors.

After entering the palace, there was a walkway passage to the king's court. Rajat looked around carefully to spot a picture of the eye. But there was nothing. He scanned the palace inside out, still there was nothing. As he was walking out, he saw a picture of the King. He looked at it closely. On the top right side of the picture, there was a blue triangle. The eye inside it was wide open. The description in the affidavit was very similar to what it looked like. It was the same eye Rajat was looking for.

The mystical picture of an eye, was now looking at Rajat. And Rajat's eyes were transfixed on it as well. At that moment, Rajat got the despairing feeling that something was not right.

He tried to find more about that picture or about that eye. He found some words inscribed just below the picture: the king with his Agha Netra. Rajat googled the word and found that in Sanskrit, the meaning of Agha Netra was the evil eye. Here was the first claim made by Shivpal which had come true. And that moment, Rajat started to worry as his first option to dismiss the plea that there was no such thing as the evil eye, proved wrong. He looked around to know more about the eye, but nothing was mentioned apart from the same word repeated twice – Agha Netra. He took a picture of the King's portrait and the inscription below it.

Rajat looked around the palace for a while and then returned to college to pick up his files. On the way back, the idea of looking for some information in the Mussoorie Library about struck him. The problem was that one would have to look though all the books in the library. He swiftly went inside the library to find a way to get a book about Agha Netra. But searching for a particular book in the Mussoorie Library was like looking for a needle in a haystack. So he Googled to find a book regarding Agha Netra, but he had no luck. Frustrated and tired, Rajat left the library and returned to the college. Unfortunately, it was too late. The college was closed, and his files were in the staff room.

Rajat drove back home empty-handed. He had no luck about the evil eye, and he had no court case files to read that night. He reached Gandhi Chowk, slowing down because of the traffic. Suddenly someone shouted his name. He looked around and saw a lean girl wearing a formal suit and a red helmet, waving at him. Then the girl waved to him to come to pull over, which he did.

They both stopped at the side of the road. The girl took off the helmet; it was Sana. Rajat was a little surprised.

"I didn't expect to see you so formally dressed in a suit and tie. What's up?" Rajat looked at Sana.

"Didn't Alisha tell you about me? I work at the Golden Gate Hotel. I have come straight from work. But leave that, tell me did you guys finally meet?" Sana asked.

Rajat was puzzled; he was almost about to ask whom she was talking about when it struck him that she was talking about Alisha who had met Kevin.

He replied quickly, "Yeah, we met at Gully's."

"And she told you all about her?"

Rajat nodded and remained quiet.

"Rajat, I will tell you what Alisha and her mother has gone through in the last couple of years. It was a challenging period for both of them, and the worst was her condition. And I know she only wants you to keep the secret to yourself, which I hope you will do for her as a favour."

Rajat stood quietly and nodded again.

Sana was worried about Alisha.

"I am not sure what came to Alisha's mind to tell you all about her face blindness. I don't know what you feel about her and her condition, but I don't want Alisha to get hurt. Her problem is she thinks too much, and she feels things too deeply. And that is a deadly combination for her condition. So, I will not ask what happened at the coffee table, but promise me that you will do what is good for Alisha. The bare minimum would be to keep the secret of her condition to yourself," Sana said worryingly.

"I promise you I won't break her trust in me," Rajat reassured her. But he knew deep in his heart how wrong it was to lie when he had already broken her trust, by asking Kevin to impersonate him.

"Thanks, Rajat. I wanted to hear that."

Sana smiled and left Rajat wondering whether he should still doubt Alisha face blindness. He asked himself the moot question: *who failed if Alisha passed the litmus test? He, himself?*

Once Sana left, Rajat took out his phone and dialled a number.

"Kevin, are you in the hotel?"

***

Rajat reached Golden Gate to meet Kevin. Kevin was in his room and was feeling dizzy after his sedative medicine. Kevin opened the door. Rajat noticed the bandage on his forehead.

"You must be having a terrible day, Kevin. What the heck happened to you?"

Kevin told him about his meeting with Alisha. He told Rajat that he slipped while coming back. Rajat, already feeling guilty having asked Kevin to impersonate him, felt he was to blame for the fall as well.

"I am not going to meet Alisha again. I did this once but no more," Kevin groaned as he lay down on the bed.

"Alisha is a simple girl, and I am breaking her trust by doing so."

Also, that he was still puzzled why Rajat asked him to impersonate him in the first place.

"I doubt that she is covering up her arrogance under the hood of face blindness," Rajat replied.

"Face what?" Kevin asked.

Rajat told Kevin about the condition.

"That makes my life simpler then. I am leaving Mussoorie in a couple of days and will never meet Alisha. And you can be you, Rajat. So, nothing changes for her," Kevin smiled.

"But now she won't believe that I am Rajat even if I tell her," Rajat said worryingly.

"Wait, you just said that she doesn't remember faces," Kevin was puzzled.

"The only way people with that condition remembers a face is by signs. Like, hair, eye colour, or birthmark on a face or a mole? These signs remain constant with that face. For example, Alisha will never recognize Sana if she stops making a ponytail and covers up that mole on her face."

"What do you want to say?" Kevin frowned.

"Alisha knows now that Rajat has a mark on his forehead. So, for her, you are Rajat, not me," Rajat smirked.

"Rajat, I am out of this. Now that is between you and Alisha. I can't betray that innocent girl. And I don't know why you want to do that to her. Just to check her arrogance? I mean, Rajat, you were never like that. Look at yourself."

Kevin was frustrated.

Rajat knew Kevin was right. But for now, he didn't have an option unless he told Alisha the truth. Unknowingly, things were changing slowly; Rajat did not want to lose Alisha. So finally, Rajat convinced Kevin to stay for a few more days till the wound healed on his forehead. Meanwhile, he would solve the MJK case. Once the mark was gone from Kevin's forehead, he could leave. Kevin agreed after much persuasion.

"So, it was a litmus test?" Kevin asked sarcastically.

Rajat nodded.

"Let me tell you what you already know. Alisha passed the test, but you my friend, failed miserably."

"Yes, indeed, Kevin. I failed," Rajat replied.

Little did they know that the scratch on Kevin's forehead would leave a deep scar in their lives in the coming days.

***

Sana reached home, and was surprised by an offer letter from Willy University in the US. Although Willy was not on her priority list, it was the first offer letter she had received from a university she had applied to. She was excited indeed, but the immediate hurdle was to arrange the money to block her seat. She told her father about the offer letter, and he promised to give her the funds, which he knew Sana would never take.

"I don't need your money, Papa. But yes, I will allow you to pay for the taxi fare when you drop me to the airport," Sana giggled and took the letter from her father.

"Is it? I thought you would like to pay the taxi fare by yourself as well," her father grinned.

"Now, don't take it to heart, Papa. And I will not apply to Willy. But I know you are proud that I am crafting the life I want on my own."

"Indeed I am. Whatever you do, you have my full support as always." Her father smiled at her.

Sana walked toward the bookshelf and put the offer letter into a book. The book next to it fell off the shelf. As Sana picked it up to place it back on the shelf, she saw a brown envelope sticking out.

"What is this, Papa?" she asked.

"This is a letter written by your grandfather on his deathbed. It has some cryptic nonsense that has no meaning." Her father came towards Sana and took the envelope.

"Can I read it?"

His father pulled out a discoloured wrinkled paper. He gently unfolded it and gave it to Sana.

She read the letter which was full of words that made no sense. At the end there was a doodle of an eye.

"What is this?"

"Forget about it. I have kept this letter safely because this was the last and the only thing he had written minutes before dying," her father replied and kept the letter back.

Sana told her father that she wanted to share the news about the offer letter with Alisha. So, she called Alisha and they decided to meet at Gully's Cafe.

Sana picked up Alisha from the college and reached Gully's the next day. She wanted to tell her that she was given the offer, but not the fact that she had decided not to accept it.

"I like your philosophy. Enjoy every happy moment of your life. No matter how big or small it is," Alisha said congratulating her.

"Life is short, so finding happiness in small moments makes it special," Sana replied. "By the way, I met Rajat yesterday."

"How was he? Was he feeling okay?" Alisha asked.

"He was good. You are asking me as if something happened to him," Sana was surprised.

Alisha told Sana about the goons who beat Rajat when they were returning from Gully's. That surprised Sana because when she met Rajat, he didn't mention the incident.

"But I didn't see anything like that on his forehead. Probably, the wound was concealed by his helmet. Surprisingly he didn't mention it," Sana was talking to herself.

Gully's Cafe was on the ground floor of a multistorey building. The building was mostly rented by offices and boutiques. When Sana and Alisha reached the cafe, it was time for most of the office staff to call it a day.

While they were still talking about what had happened the previous day, Alisha suddenly, like a bolt of lightning, felt she had seen everything around her earlier. The people, the chair, the wind and even the smell of the cafe. It was déjà vu.

She looked at Sana and then up at the floors of the building. Alisha knew she had seen the complete scene – office building, people, plants – everything around her before. She tried hard to remember where but couldn't. Sana looked at Alisha in surprise, as she suddenly looked worried and frustrated.

In a flash, trembling Alisha remembered where she has seen the entire scene. She went into deep shock as she remembered what was going to happen next. She smothered her scream with her palm. And at that very moment, a girl fell from the top of the building merely a few feet away from Alisha. A few drops of blood splattered on Sana's face. The thud of the body falling was so loud that the crowd began to run helter-skelter. Sana looked at Alisha who was frozen, staring with wide eyes and raised eyebrows at the girl's body. She yelled at Alisha and pulled her away with one hand. She managed to drag her till the parking lot. She shouted at Alisha to sit on the scooter and they drove away.

"Alisha, what was that? You reacted in shock just before she fell from the building? As if you knew this was going to happen!" Sana screamed at Alisha after they stopped in a lane.

"Can you drop me home? I am not feeling well," Alisha said in a shaky voice. The incident confirmed Alisha's dreadful dreams were going to come true in real life every time.

Chapter 11

Over to the Masters

Somewhere in Kolkata

Around nine in the morning, the phone buzzed in Sarkar House in the eastern side of Kolkata. A septuagenarian, Bijoy Sarkar, a tall man with winter white hair and sparkling eyes, picked up the receiver of a landline phone.

"He has no clue yet. We are keeping an eye on him," the voice on the other side of the phone said in a low tone.

"Almost a hundred years when it was last seen. Like a phoenix, it will rise from the ashes again. Find it before the triad finds it," Bijoy replied and hung up.

"Arinjay, that traitor!" Bijoy murmured.

Sarkar House was a house with crumbling rock walls, beautiful high arched windows, that was built almost a century ago near the banks of the Hooghly river. The house still stood tall with minor wear and tear over the years. An archaeological survey of India also found Sarkar's house to be of extreme importance, and thus they had put up a board in front of the house.

The state government convinced Bishwa Sarkar to move out of that house, but his father, Bijoy Sarkar, a man of self-respect, was unmoved. He wanted to live the rest of his life in the house and refused to move out.

The Sarkar House housed the family of Bishwa Sarkar, his wife, their two kids, and Bishwa's father Bijoy, and bedridden mother, suffering from pulmonary congestion and pneumonia. Bishwa was working in the railway as a Travelling Ticket Examiner often travelled around the eastern railways. He was the only breadwinner in the house.

Bijoy had never been uncomfortable like this before. With steady hands, he picked up the phone and dialled the number.

"We have to remain patient. The boy has just landed. Are you sure the Agha Netra is there?"

"Bijoy, the Agha Netra is incomplete without the messenger. The Triad is searching for it in Guangzhou. I got to know it's here. We have to get it before the Chinese does. And you know till what extent these guys will go to lay their hands on the Agha Netra. Protectors are eagerly waiting to reclaim it as well," the husky voice on the other side of the phone continued.

Bijoy took a deep breath, paused, and continued slowly, "Almost a hundred years have passed and no one knows where to find it. I am worried. Will we be able to hand it over to the Protectors?"

"The Agha Netra has been waiting for its protector, too, for these many years. Losing the Agha Netra by the protector has bought about the curse of the messenger. Now the eight of us have to find the ninth Unknown from outside of ourselves. The new messenger is cursed too; that person can see people but can't remember them. Once the person hands over the Agha Netra to the nine, the person should not remember them. The situation is critical. With the Agha Netra I am hopeful that a new messenger will also be found. Bijoy, be ready to find the Agha Netra and hand it over to the new messenger," the voice coughed and hung up.

Sarkar House had a storeroom packed with old boxes, scripts wrapped in cloth, and cartons. The walls of the rooms were moist and damp, and the odour of the dampness had kept Bijoy away from going inside. Bishwa and his wife never entered the room for fear of snakes and other creatures that might roam around on the floor. They often spotted a few of them at the entrance of the room. As a kid, Bijoy used to often go into that room with his father. The last time his father got a glimpse of the

Agha Netra in that room, but now there was only a grooved case where his father used to keep the Agha Netra. Bijoy walked into the room and was nostalgic, remembering his father. He sat on a chair after brushing off the thick layer of dust from it. He looked at the small cloud in the sky through the ventilation window and remembered a story which his father told him about the Agha Netra. The story where trust was broken, and the Agha Netra was lost forever in oblivion.

***

Mussoorie's cold weather was aggravating the pain of Kevin's wound. So he decided to stay at the hotel for a few days. He had taken a month off for the purpose he was there. So, while waiting for his masala tea at the cafe of the hotel, he googled a few places around Mussoorie.

"How are you doing, sir? You must be in pain judging by the bandage on your head," Sana said as she walked towards Kevin.

"You don't often get such souvenirs in a tourist place," Kevin replied sarcastically.

"Sorry if I hurt you by asking about it, sir," Sana said.

"No, not at all. It was just a joke," Kevin smiled and continued, "And on the contrary, it feels good if someone asks about you when you are in pain."

"You feel better soon, sir," Sana replied.

"You know what, I almost forgot about the pain in the last couple of minutes. I am sure that if you have a cup of tea with me, I will feel better."

Kevin looked at Sana.

"I am not allowed to sit with our guests, sir," Sana apologized.

Kevin got up from his seat.

"Forget that word, sir, and be my guest today. Please."

Sana smiled and said, "Okay, if you say so."

Kevin replied, "Thank you, and by the way, they say there is a lot that can happen over coffee. But I have more faith in tea."

Sana and Kevin chuckled.

The aroma of the tea from the hot cup was rejuvenating, so much so that it fuelled their conversation long enough to qualify as a date, which it was not.

"Why are you here, Kevin?" Sana asked, holding the cup of tea. Even though Kevin was not ready to give an honest answer, he did not want to sound sheepish.

"I have some personal work here. I don't know how long it will take to complete it, but have a month to fulfil my commitment."

Kevin sipped the tea and held the cup with both palms overlapping the cup to warm them.

"If I could be of any help, do tell me. By the way, do you have any friends here? I am sure there is the one you met at the cafe," Sana smiled.

"That cafe meeting was for my work. So no, I have no friends here. "

Kevin paused and looked at Sana and continued,

"Will you be my friend or a guide?"

"I choose my friends, and they are very special. And very close to me. For you, let's start by being a guide." Sana smiled.

"I am obliged. I want to look around shops which sell antiques. So tag along with me this coming Sunday for window shopping," Kevin requested Sana.

She agreed. After spending almost an hour and drinking two more cups of masala tea, Sana left.

As soon as she left, Kevin took out the phone and texted a message to someone.

There will be someone with me next time. Stay away! She is important for this job to be completed.

***

On the other side of the city. Rajat was getting anxious about the symbol of the eye. Visiting the library in Mussoorie was part of his routine now. He scanned every page available on Google searches, websites, journals, and books. Unfortunately, the only similar image that related to the symbol was of the Illuminati. The eye symbol and Illuminati were identical in demonstrating the importance of the eye, but it was not the same.One day, after days of unfruitful visits to the library, he was flipping pages of a book talking about a secret society in India. An old man in his late sixties, with white hair and a slightly bent shoulder, walked past Rajat and looked at him from the corner of his eyes. He spotted something, turned back, and stood behind Rajat.

"I have never seen anyone reading about the secret society so intently. Are you doing some research on it, or is it for fun?" the man asked curiously.

"These eyes are looking for an eye," Rajat smirked and replied cryptically, pointing his hand towards his eyes.

"I can't think of anything other than the Illuminati. But it's not a secret. It's pretty open in the public domain now. And that is not in the pages of this book," he said.

"Illuminati. Yes, I know about it. But what I am searching for is similar to that," Rajat replied.

The old man frowned, and he pulled a ballpoint pen from his pocket. Then he pulled a newspaper lying in front of Rajat and scribbled something on the empty space. Finally, he turned the page to Rajat and pointed at that doodle.

"Does it look something similar to this?"

Rajat looked and was stunned to see the eye. He exclaimed, "Yes, it is! It looks quite similar to what I am looking for."

The old man tore the part where he had drawn the doodle and tossed it in the dustbin. He kept both hands on the table and said,

"My son! As far as I know, I am the only one who can tell you a little about it. It might be an introduction. But I want to save those words for other things. So, I can only give you a two-word answer. Stay away."

"Why? Please help me. You are the first one I met who knows something," Rajat begged.

"Who are you? Why are you searching for it?"

Rajat paused and decided not to tell him the truth.

"I am a student. I saw this symbol in the palace, so it triggered curiosity my curiosity," Rajat replied.

The sparkling eyes of the old man were looking intently at Rajat.

"I can see in your eyes, son. And I know it's not about curiosity. Best of luck!"

And he walked out of the library.

Rajat was not able to stop him. But when he left the building, he inquired about him and got to know he had been talking to the librarian Joy Ghosh, whom the staff often referred to as a human encyclopaedia.

***

The MJK board members were becoming anxious about the progress of the case. The trustees expected the college board to start building a new campus as soon as they won the case. But this new twist of Shivpal was testing their patience. And Rajat, who was not keeping them updated, was adding fuel to their anxiousness. Rajat was asked to meet the MJK board and present the progress. First, and most importantly, about the next steps of action on the appeal made by Shivpal.

He reached the meeting room. There were few members only, including his uncle, a trustee in the college.

"Take your seat, Rajat," his uncle pointed his finger to a chair close to him.

Rajat briskly walked and sat on the chair. He kept his briefcase on the table.

"I don't want to see any documents. Let's come straight to the point," he said before continuing, "Rajat, what do you feel about this case? Can we win it?"

"Yes indeed, uncle," he paused and said, "Sorry, sir."

"Okay. The trust that I bestowed upon you carries respect. I have heard that you are hunting voraciously for something mythological. Is it true?"

Rajat remained quiet for a few seconds.

"Yes. I have to get to the core of the matter. And Shivpal—"

His uncle stopped him.

"We expect each college student to scientifically reason anything in their daily life. Facts and reality drive thought. Imagine someone is fighting a case on behalf of MJK on the basis of a mythological subject. And not through the rational use of laws."

"But—" Rajat said, and he was stopped again by his uncle.

"I will give you two months, son. If, during this time, the progress is impressive enough to win the case, you stay. Else, I heard that you want to go back to Kolkata and start your own law firm. I will not get in your way."

Saying that, his uncle walked out of the room.

Rajat was disappointed that he had not been given the freedom to fight the battle. The next two months would be crucial for him to close the case.

It had been a long time since he visited the MJK canteen. He decided to have a cup of tea at the canteen and ponder about what to do next.

He reached the canteen and saw Alisha sitting at a table. Rajat was not ready to face her after what he had done to her.

After placing the order for tea at the counter, he sat next to Alisha's table quietly.

Rajat pretended to text someone on his phone as he looked at Alisha. She looked different. That girl had gone through so much pain in her life, and now was struggling with the medical condition. Still, she smiled because she knew what pain was. Her prettiness was just a bonus, as her inner beauty was the most stunning. Looking at her, Rajat forgot all his worries, the meeting he just had, and the two-month deadline. She looked magical.

Alisha saw someone was looking at her mysteriously. It was annoying, and she felt uncomfortable.

"Hello, do I know you?" she asked sharply.

Rajat got a jolt.

"No, I don't think so," he stammered.

Alisha remained quiet and tried to remember where she had heard this voice. It sounded familiar.

"I think I know you, but I can't remember," Alisha added.

"Sorry, I don't remember meeting you., God knows I would never forget your beautiful face, if I had met you," Rajat smiled.

Alisha smirked; it was a compliment she could never give to anyone. Looking at Rajat, she said,

"I am Alisha and I work here."

"I am Kevin. I came here to meet someone in the college," Rajat said lowly, wondering about how often he'd have to hide his identity from Alisha.

"You were looking at me as if you know me," Alisha asked suspiciously.

"Or, you might be the most beautiful girl in the college. And I can't take my eyes off you." Rajat was spontaneous in his response. He dared to speak his heart out because he knew Alisha would not remember his face.

Alisha felt annoyed, "I think you are going too fast, Kevin."

She got up and walked towards her lab.

"Look, I am sorry, Alisha," Rajat said.

Alisha again turned back momentarily as if trying to recall where she had heard the voice before.

Rajat felt for the first time that he was falling for her.

The next day, Rajat returned to the library again. This time in search of Joy Ghosh. After a couple of hours, he saw Joy Ghosh walking down the corridor unsteadily. Rajat swiftly went up to him.

"I need to solve the mystery of the eye symbol. I am losing my sleep over it."

Joy stopped, turned back to Rajat and smiled.

"Curiosity makes one happy; because you are learning and discovering each moment, that you are curious. Your eyes are tired searching for what I saw that day. That indicates that you are not curious but frustrated. You are looking for the eye for a purpose."

"I won't hide from you. I am here to fight a legal battle for MJK, and it has come to a point where I desperately need to find the truth. I saw it in the painting in the palace. Is that eye for real?" Rajat was anxious.

"Yes, it existed. But the one you saw in the painting was not there a few days ago. Someone drew it there for a purpose," Joy said.

"What? Why? I want to know more. Please help me," Rajat begged.

Joy looked at Rajat and said.

"Come with me."

And navigating through the tall bookshelves packed with books, they reached the table which Joy called his small cubical.

He pulled out one chair and asked Rajat to sit down. Joy sat right opposite him.

"You know Rajat, the belief in the eye is ancient and ubiquitous; evidence of it is found in ancient Greece and Rome, in Jewish, Islamic, Buddhist, and Hindu traditions. We all know about Shiva's third eye, but do you know that 'bindi' stems from the Sanskrit word 'bindu' which means 'drop'. Around 3000 BC, when the rishi wrote the Vedas, they mentioned the seven chakras. The sixth chakra is precisely where the bindi is placed. This is again the very same place where the third eye of Shiva is located. An ancient Egyptian symbol, the Eye of Horus, symbolizes protection and well-being. For centuries, the eye has been a symbol of protection and devastation in many senses."

Joy was entirely in his element while explaining the concept of the eye symbols to Rajat.

"Coming to the 21st century, people still use it for protection. In today's world, people don't feel shy about placing a symbol or face with big eyes in today's modern homes to protect the family from evil."

Joy smiled and looked at him.

Rajat had been so engrossed in looking for that specific eye symbol that he completely forgot there were so many places where he had seen the eye.

Joy saw Rajat lost in thoughts about the eye, so he snapped his fingers to bring him back.

Rajat sat up with a start. Joy said in a low voice, "Now let's come to your curiosity. The eye symbol you are desperate to find."

He walked towards the blackboard nearby and wrote in capital letters:

A-G-H-A N-E-T-R-A

Joy turned back to Rajat.

"'Agha' means 'bad' or 'evil'. And 'Netra' means 'eye'. So combined, it means evil eye. There is a mythological belief that this eye is protecting something. It is not alone, but it is attached to something. Just like the eye is placed it in front of a house, book, or something else to symbolize protection. But whatever it is protecting, that thing should not be opened or explored. Else, there will be a holocaust in waiting."

Joy took a deep breath.

"I told you to stay away because this is cursed for the one who breaks into what it is protecting."

Rajat was astonished.

"But where I can find it," he asked.

Joy smiled and replied.

"Only evidence of that eye last seen was in Xiamen."

"Xiamen?"

"It's in China," Joy replied.

"How are you so sure it's in Xiamen and not here?" Rajat was doubtful.

"There was a time when I was researching the subject. I read about triads who were somehow connected to the eye. There were groups like Zinka, Kingla many other tribes that were treasure hunters. You can find books about them in our library as well. In today's world these tribes have merged into civil society. Then I stumbled upon a piece of news where a mysterious killing was reported in Xiamen. The murdered man had a tattoo of exact same eye drawn on his arm. Everyone thought that there was some connection with the eye. But like any other news, it faded away into oblivion," Joy said.

"That is interesting," said Rajat as he took in the information.

"So, it's not here, unless you want to go to China and find out."

It was disappointing news for Rajat. A dead end. He thanked Joy for his time and walked out of the library. Worried, he WhatsApped Kevin and told him that he was coming down to meet him.

***

Alisha had not slept since the last few nights. It was the fear of dreaming something dreadful that kept her sleep-deprived. The lack of sleep was making her life miserable.

Her mother took Alisha's head on her lap and tapped her forehead gently.

"You need to sleep, Alisha. Not all your dreams will come true. Have faith in God. There might be a purpose behind all this. You never know," her mother pacified her.

"What is the use if I don't remember the faces? These people walk in front of me, and a few minutes later, they die. I can't even help them. I can't stop them from dying. It is a curse. I feel cursed," she sobbed.

"Everything happens for a reason, Alisha."

Her mother kept massaging her head and running her fingers through her hair, hoping to ease her pain.

After a few minutes, there was no response from Alisha. Her mother looked down and saw her sleeping like a baby, peacefully and undisturbed, embraced by the gentle arms of slumber. Her mother remained as she was for the next few hours to ensure Alisha didn't wake up. And true enough, Alisha didn't wake up that night.

The next day Alisha was sitting at the breakfast table, looking at her palm and rotating her wrist, as if she was trying to find something on her hand.

"What happened, Alisha? Go and wash your hand if you feel it is not clean."

"Last night, I saw something unique in my dream," Alisha said in a low voice.

Her mother reached her worryingly, "What did you see? I told you every dream—"

Alisha cut her mother short.

"I saw someone giving me a box with blood-soaked hands. And as I took the box from the person, I felt my hand wet and warm as if I had dipped it in a bowl of lukewarm water. And I walked away from him." She paused.

"But I didn't wake up," she added.

Alisha was lost staring at her hands with her eyes wide open.

Alisha's behaviour was worrying her mother. She thought if she did not consult a doctor soon, Alisha would lose her mind. How long could the poor girl handle all these things? It was taking a toll on her health.

"Why don't you take a day off from college? Spend some time with Sana," her mother said.

Alisha looking at her hand, lost in her own thoughts.

"Yes, you are right. I need a break," Alisha agreed and took out her phone.

Sana called her to the Golden Gate Hotel so she could spend some time with Alisha while she was at work. The cafeteria of the hotel was just behind the reception. It would be easy for Sana to quickly walk out in case she was needed at the reception desk.

"You're feeling low nowadays, Alisha. Trust me, at this age, you should be shopping to get yourself out of being despondent. The other option is to have a boyfriend," Sana chuckled.

Alisha smiled. "It's not that I am feeling low or dejected. But I feel helpless and in pain. You know I'm not too fond of shopping," she giggled.

"And as far as having a boyfriend is concerned, you know I have trust issues about the face. But you know what. Yesterday something interesting happened. There was this guy in the canteen, and he was flirting with me at the first 'hello.'"

"Seriously, that strange. How does he look?" Sana asked.

Alisha shook her head and rolled her eyes.

"Like a mannequin!"

"Ah, my bad, the faces you don't remember. But frankly, every girl should have that blessing. So that your commitment is not at stake because you can forget people's faces anytime," Sana chuckled.

"And to give that advice, I have a friend like you!" Alisha smirked and continued. "But you know what, I felt that I have heard his voice before."

"You did? Did he tell you his name?"

"He said, his name was Kevin."

"Oh! That's strange! I, too, know someone here in the hotel with the same name," Sana said.

"You're sure it was not Rajat in college?"

"No, he was not Rajat. He wouldn't say something like that. And overall, it's easy for me to spot him with that bandage on his forehead." Alisha leaned back on the sofa and frowned.

"Here is my Byomkesh Bakshi," Sana said, and they both laughed.

"Okay listen, you wait here. I will be back shortly," Sana told Alisha as she had to be at the reception for some urgent work.

Meanwhile, Rajat reached the hotel and walked into Kevin's room.

"You look tired; what happened?" Kevin asked Rajat as he sat on the sofa.

"I am lost. Frankly, it's like I am aimlessly wandering. I am drained mentally and physically; I am tired of searching," Rajat blabbered.

"Hold on, hold on. You need a break! Let's get some coffee at the cafe downstairs."

Kevin walked toward Rajat and tapped his shoulder. Since Rajat met Joy and found out that the Agha Netra was in China, he was not in a mood to think. So, he just followed Kevin to the cafe.

Kevin stepped inside the cafe and was a few metres ahead of Rajat. As soon as he reached a table, a voice called out.

"Rajat?"

Kevin turned and saw Alisha looking at him and waving her hand. He was stunned to see Alisha there. He waved back.

Rajat saw that scene unfold from a few metres away. And he quickly turned back to step out of the cafe. He pulled out his phone and texted Kevin,

I know Alisha saw you; come out. I am waiting outside.

Rajat kept his phone away and saw Sana standing in front of him.

"Hello! What you are doing here? And where is your bandage? Looks like you are better," Sana said though she was surprised to see Rajat in the hotel.

"I was here to meet my friend. But unfortunately, he left early. So now, I will have to meet him elsewhere"

"He is my guest. Which room he is in?"

"I forgot. Anyway, I need to rush. See you soon, Sana."

While Rajat was talking to Sana, at the cafe Alisha was talking to Kevin.

"Nice to see you. Honestly, I didn't expect to see you here," Kevin said.

"Sana works here, so I thought of meeting her at the hotel," Alisha replied and smiled.

"That's nice. Unfortunately, I have to rush. I was here to meet my friend, but he left the hotel early. Sorry I have to leave," Kevin said.

"It's fine, Rajat. I have company. See you in college."

As Kevin rushed outside, he bumped into Sana near the reception.

"Hey Kevin!" Sana shouted.

"Hey Sana, let me catch up with you later; I need to meet someone," Kevin smiled and walked out briskly.

Sana was baffled to see Kevin rushing out. After a few minutes, she went back to the cafe.

"You know Rajat was here."

"Yeah, I met him," Alisha smiled

"But how did you recognize him?" Sana asked.

"Now, don't start that again," Alisha chuckled and handed over the cup of coffee to Sana.

"But Alisha, I want to know how you recognized him." Sana was curious.

"I told you about that bandage," Alisha said.

Sana murmured to herself, *"Bandage? Is someone impersonating Rajat? Is it Kevin?"*

Kevin came out of the hotel and found Rajat standing near his motorcycle.

"That was close," Kevin rushed toward Rajat worryingly.

"Don't worry. I told Sana I came to meet someone in the hotel but he left the hotel early."

"To whom?" Kevin was puzzled and continued, "I told the same story to Alisha."

"Sana. She works at the reception. A very close friend of Alisha. Have you met Sana before?" Rajat asked and started his motorcycle.

"No," Kevin replied, sitting as pillion on the motorcycle.

"Where are we going?"

"Gully's. I need a break," Rajat said and accelerated the motorcycle through the lanes of Mussoorie.

"Rajat, wait! There is a yellow 'Caution Do Not Enter Barricade' tape! Something must have happened."

They saw that the tape barricaded a small area of the cafe. So Rajat asked one person passing by about the scene. They learned that a girl had fallen from the top floor. The police were investigating it as murder.

As the cafe was closed, they started to walk to the nearby park.

"So, Kevin, why are you still here? I know I asked you to stay but you should be getting back to work by now."

Rajat looked at Kevin while walking down the street.

"What happened to you, Rajat? A few days back, you were begging me to stay. And now you're asking me why I am here!" Kevin said in frustration.

"Please don't take it otherwise. I am just being more cautious, as you are here because of me. You should go back. I will handle the situation with Alisha. Come, let's walk to that bench," Rajat said pointing to a bench near the park.

Kevin didn't see this coming. He had not even started the work for which he was in Mussoorie. At that moment, he decided that he would soon find a new reason to stay back.

The Mussoorie weather was changing slowly as secrets among close friends was filling the air. Sana knew that who Alisha was meeting was not Rajat. And, Kevin was hiding the reason for his stay in Mussoorie from Rajat.

The close ones were sowing the seeds of doubt, unaware they would sour their relationships one day.

Chapter 12

Tour around the City

Close friends can become strangers with your secrets in the snap of a finger.

Kevin was at the hotel café waiting for Sana. She promised to show Kevin around Mussoorie, specifically around the places where most of the antiques were sold. People bought antiques as souvenirs, and although she didn't really care about them, it was a promise she had made to Kevin and did not want to break.

While at the cafe, Kevin pulled out his phone and opened a photo of a sketch from his picture gallery. He remembered the moment he drew the picture when he was in Kolkata. The reason why he was here… searching for a box.

Few months ago in Kolkata

Kevin reached the bungalow in old north Kolkata near Cossipore. Staying primarily in new Kolkata, Kevin had never got a chance to visit the area. The Sarbamangala Temple was one of the few known places in the area. The reason for the trip was that only Maa Sarbmangala could help him at that point.

The façade of the bungalow had yellow walls with beautiful red lines presenting botanical painting of plants with bright red flowers and sulphur yellow dots. Two guards escorted him to a small hall where Bijoy was waiting for him. He walked toward Kevin and showed him a photo of the box of the Agha Netra.

"Let's come to the point. Take the pen and paper and draw this image. This box is in Mussoorie. The last time it was seen, it was almost a hundred years back, around the time when the Indian freedom struggle was going on."

Kevin took the paper and sketched the box. It was not difficult to draw. After a few minutes, when he finished, Bijoy took the paper and looked at it.

"I must say, you are good at sketching," he said and smiled.

Kevin was afraid and still not aware of what was coming his way.

"Son, we have your life in our claws. The debt you owe is one you can't repay. But this is a chance you've got. You need to find this box for us," Bijoy smiled and said.

"As you don't have a choice to say yes or no, let me explain the rules of this treasure hunt. First, you will not speak about this to anyone; these two boys behind you are my eyes."

Bijoy pointed his finger toward the man who had escorted Kevin to the bungalow.

"Second, you have only a month to find it."

Kevin asked nervously, "What's inside the box?"

"Don't worry about it, son. Bring that box to us, and you are free from your debt."

Even though Bijoy had a dreadful voice, he was not being authoritative because he knew Kevin didn't have a choice.

He signalled to his bodyguards to escort Kevin out. The meeting ended in less than fifteen minutes. Kevin was standing outside the bungalow with a piece of paper in his hand. That A4 sheet of paper was his only way to freedom from debt and a new life.

Present

Kevin heard a hand clap, and he woke up from the memory lanes of Kolkata and his meeting with Bijoy. He saw Sana standing in front of him.

"You were lost; everything okay?"

Kevin swiftly put off the phone and kept it in his pocket.

"I was thinking how best I can keep you happy and not bore you with my company today."

Sana laughed.

"It's not that difficult a task. Let me help you here. I like talking. Talking a lot."

Kevin exhaled and frowned.

"And I love listening a lot. It's a good start."

They both giggled.

Sana liked Kevin's sense of humour. Since they met the first time, they had hit it off instantly. It felt like they had always known each other. Kevin on the other hand forgot all his cares when he met Sana. He liked who he was when he was with her.

"Tell me, why are you fishing around for antiques?" Sana asked curiously.

"I recently started to develop it as my hobby," Kevin replied.

They spent some time looking around the shops of Mussoorie. Kevin wasn't too hopeful and knew he was searching for a needle in the haystack. Sana liked how Kevin looked at the antique objects; she had never seen such curiosity in someone before.

After a long search around different shops, Kevin was losing his patience. But the most challenging part was not to vent out his frustration in front of her.

"Don't you think you owe me some tea after this tiring search?" Sana smirked.

"I'm so sorry, my bad," Kevin replied. After a few minutes, they stopped at a cafe.

"You know what? I like your sense of humour," Sana said sipping her cup of tea.

"I will take it as appreciation," Kevin smiled and continued. "But I don't rank myself good at making friends. It's hard to find someone who likes you the way you are."

"I agree and for the same reason, I have many friends but only a few close ones," Sana said.

"Like marriages, I strongly believe that friendships are also made in heaven," Kevin stated sipping the hot tea.

"I like that, and can't agree more!" Sana giggled.

Kevin didn't remember the last he had such a good time. He hoped the tea would never finish, and they would keep talking.

Sana, on the other hand, wanted to understand Kevin better. She felt that there was a lot Kevin was hiding. What he revealed about himself might be only the tip of an iceberg.

"The weather wants me to stay for longer in this coffee shop," Kevin said.

"I was expecting some other reason. Let me give you another chance," Sana said to a baffled Kevin.

He replied, "Or it's your company."

"I liked the latter reason, Mr Kevin." Sana smiled at him.

"Me too," Kevin smiled, looking down at the tea.

***

In Mussoorie's cold weather, the tea at the MJK canteen was the most sought after. In a day, there were few hours when the canteen was less crowded, and Alisha liked to be at the canteen then.

Rajat walked into the canteen with a bunch of papers in his hand, one of which had a doodle of the Agha Netra. While briskly walking inside, he saw Alisha sitting in the corner in a white kurta and a red dupatta. Day by day, it was becoming difficult for Rajat to take his eyes off Alisha. Rajat was still unable to figure out if it was her innocent soul and how she quietly struggled daily in the faceless world, or was it her beauty which drew him to her.

Looking at her, he decided to continue the Kevin episode, so he walked toward Alisha, pulled the chair, and sat in front of her.

"Let me guess, you like to dive into deep thoughts when you are in the canteen?" Rajat said in a slightly loud voice, startling Alisha.

"Sorry, do I know you?" Alisha replied in a low voice, puzzled, looking at Rajat.

"I am Kevin; I met you a few days back in the canteen."

Kevin smiled.

Alisha rolled up her eyes.

"What are you doing in MJK? You don't look like a student to me."

"Nope, I am not a student," Rajat said and kept his papers on the table.

"I am getting help from a few college students for my research."

"Strange, I have never heard of that before." Alisha didn't look convinced by that response.

"You need another cup of tea to explain what I do. Would you mind if I get one for you?" Rajat requested Alisha, pointing his fingers to the empty cup. He prayed that Alisha would say yes and he would get some time to spend with her.

Alisha could not say no to that request, and Rajat told Aru to bring two cups of tea.

It was not difficult for Rajat to come up with a story around research work. The conversation lasted more than two cups. And Alisha, unaware of the time, sat sitting and chatting with Rajat.

"I must leave for my lab. Class is starting in a few minutes," Alisha said as she looked at her watch.

"Yes, work comes first. I respect that. Hope to see you someday again." Rajat smiled and extended his hand for a handshake. While extending his hand, a couple of sheets of paper from his bundle fell to the ground. The one that landed near Alisha had the doodle on it. She swiftly picked up the paper, and her eyes were glued to the Agha Netra.

Alisha suddenly looked uneasy. It was the same eye engraved on the box she had seen in her dream.

"Is this image part of your research?" Alisha said worryingly while handing over the paper to Rajat.

"Yes, currently the mystery of my life."

Rajat took a deep breath and rolled up the paper.

"You looked puzzled. Have you seen this somewhere?" Rajat asked looking at her worried face.

"No, I have never seen it before," Alisha said in a stammering voice, and before Rajat could ask her what happened, she rushed out of the canteen.

Rajat felt that something was not right with Alisha. He wondered if it was because of the Agha Netra or was there something else bothering her?

***

The image of the eye and Kevin together was not a good sign for Alisha.

Was Kevin holding that box in his blood-drenched hand? Was he the one who was going to die?

That evening, Alisha's mind was consumed by thoughts of the mysterious box. Lost in deep contemplation, she wondered about the box and the hand and moreover, about the deep impact it was having in her life.

"How long has it been since I last saw you laugh?" Alisha's mother said at the dinner table.

"I don't feel like going out, Ma. I don't want to meet people," Alisha said, scooping some rice pudding with a spoon.

"That will worry me more. You cannot stay like this. I told you the dreams would never come true again," Alisha's mother said.

"I met a guy in the canteen. He had an image of an eye drawn on the paper. It was the same as the one I had seen in my dream. Kevin may be the next one to die."

Alisha looked at her mother, and a tear rolled down her left cheek.

Alisha's mother swiftly got up and wiped her tears.

"Don't cry, Alisha. It will make you weak," her mother consoled her.

"But this time, I have decided, no matter what happens, I will not let him die. This time I will turn this curse of dreams into a blessing!"

Alisha looked at her mother and said, "Kevin will not die." And she smiled.

***

Since Rajat learned that the Agha Netra was last seen in China, he had lost all hope. But a thought twitching in his mind was why he was investing all his energy in looking for that eye, what he would get in the end? Would it help him win the case? He could win the case with better arguments and scientific reasoning. His uncle too seemed to have no faith in him. So, winning the case and getting his trust back was more vital than searching for that box.

He decided that before he called off his search for the Agha Netra, he would let Joy know about it. Rajat headed for the library to thank Joy. He was not there at his desk. Instead, he saw a man clearing his desk and arranging all of Joy's stuff in the cupboard.

"When will Joy come to the library?" Rajat asked.

The man paused, looked at Rajat with tearful eyes for a few seconds and said,

"Never"

"Sorry, I didn't get that." Rajat was baffled.

"Joy died two days back. Someone poisoned him. Such a nice soul. He departed too soon," the man replied tearfully.

The news hit Rajat like a thud in his chest. He was shocked and petrified.

The man said, "The doctor has taken his body for postmortem. If you want to know more, you can take the medical report from the police." The man looked at Rajat for a few seconds and went to a different section.

Rajat stood frozen in shock. And his thoughts went silent except for one thing that kept banging in his mind, "Why would someone poison him?"

In that silence, he reached the police station to learn more about what had happened. Unfortunately, the police station had few constables and only one sub-inspector present.

Rajat tapped the shoulder of a constable.

"I want to know what happened to Joy Ghosh. How did he die?"

The constable was flipping pages of a file. Without looking up, he said,

"Who? That librarian?"

"Yes, the old man."

The constables looked at Rajat from top to bottom and said,

"He was poisoned. And strangely, with a poison made with Chinese herbs, according to the report. We all know the quality of Chinese products, wonder how this was so strong," he smirked.

While Rajat was standing and listening to what the constable was saying to him, the sub-inspector walked in.

"Who are you?"

"I am Rajat. I had met Joy a few days back. It's shocking to learn about his death," Rajat said in a low voice.

"You are Rajat? We got something from Joy's pocket. See, if it was meant for you," saying this the sub-inspector walked inside his office. Rajat followed him.

He handed over a chit to Rajat. It read:

'Rajat, I was wrong. It is here. After you read this note, shred it and burn it.'

Rajat was baffled for a few minutes, and then suddenly the message dawned on him.

"In case you have any clue or any information, share it with us as it will help us," the sub-inspector said.

That note revealed Agha Netra was there. In Mussoorie itself.

"Look, Rajat. Joy's death is not natural, and this note is from his pocket. If it was written for you, then we will need to ask you to come in for questioning," the Inspector said, looking at the piece of paper.

Rajat nodded and came out of the police station worried. He had come to meet Joy to inform him about giving up on the Agha Netra. But it seems like the Agha Netra didn't want to leave Rajat.

The earlier speculation that the Agha Netra was in Xiamen, and that later he was killed by Chinese poison were concerning. There was definitely a link with the Chinese.

Rajat came out of the police station pondering. Should he quit the search for the Agha Netra and focus on his case? Or should he finish the quest for the eye? Suddenly he received a message.

'The Board wants to know the progress of the case. You update Mr Shukla about it tomorrow in college. If the board decides to meet you, there will be a board meeting next week. Just drop by the college tomorrow.'

Chapter 13

Trust Issues

The next afternoon Rajat reached college and told Shukla that there had not been much progress. He would file an affidavit next week to get a new date from the court.

Shukla, personal assistant to the principal, was unhappy with the news. He warned Rajat that the board might call him next week if he didn't have something to show. Disappointed, Rajat reached the canteen to calm himself. He knew the thoughts in his mind were like flowing water. When the mind is turbulent, it isn't easy to see correctly, but when it became clear, one could make the correct decisions.

Alisha wanted to meet Kevin in the canteen. This time she had a bracelet to gift him. That was the only way she could identify Kevin, among others. Again, she was hoping Kevin would recognize her in the canteen. Alisha, for once, wanted to save someone from dying. She was adamant that she would save Kevin.

Rajat saw Alisha in the canteen looking unsettled. He waited and then walked up to her.

"You look worried. Everything okay with you?" Rajat asked.

Alisha looked at him for a moment, paused, and asked in a low voice. "Kevin?"

"Of course, I am Kevin," Rajat blurted out almost forgetting that he was impersonating his friend.

"Thank god you are here." She folded her hands looking at the ceiling.

"What happened?" Rajat asked surprised at that reaction.

She pulled his hand towards him without saying a word and tied the bracelet around his wrist.

"Do not take it off."

Rajat was even more baffled.

"Alisha, what happened?"

"This will help me to recognize you and will keep you alive. Promise me you won't take it off."

Rajat didn't know how to react. First, he waited and let Alisha settle down. Then, he pulled up a chair and asked Alisha what had happened.

"Well, I see dreadful dreams which always come true. I saw you dying this time, and I promised myself I wouldn't let this happen."

"Well, and you think it was me?" Rajat asked.

"Yes, in my dream, I saw a box with the same eye engraved. Someone was holding that box with hands drenched in blood," Alisha said worryingly. "Are you searching for a box with an eye on it?"

Rajat was shocked to hear Alisha's words, but he didn't let his emotions show. He nodded his head slowly.

Alisha smiled. "I hope you will keep this bracelet."

"Alisha, may I ask you something?" Rajat asked in a low voice.

"What it is?" Alisha said while looking at the bracelet.

"If you come to know that someone has betrayed you, that he has made fun of your weakness behind your back and even used it for selfish interests, and then you see that he was going to die in your dream. Would you still save his life? Would you still ask him to wear this bracelet?" Rajat stuttered.

"That would mean I trusted him blindly," she replied.

Rajat nodded.

"That would be the saddest part of my life, Kevin. The man whom I trusted and perhaps loved too had betrayed me. Love will surely turn into hate. But you know what, he who doesn't love or trust himself is bound to mistreat women who trust him."

Alisha smiled sadly.

"Still, I will do what I can to save his life," she added.

Rajat smiled back.

"Thank you for this bracelet."

After Alisha left, he looked at the bracelet and gently kissed it.

"Sorry, Alisha. I am really sorry."

The news of Joy's death was in the local newspaper. Kevin read the article while sipping his morning coffee and was surprised by the fact that someone had used Chinese poison to kill in Mussoorie. Meeting Sana at the coffee table in the hotel café had become routine for him.

"May I ask you something?" Sana asked.

"Yes?" Kevin replied.

"What exactly are you looking for in the antique shops?" Sana asked, keeping the coffee mug on the table.

"There is something important in my life. But, unfortunately, I can only tell you that much." Kevin pursed his lips.

"I believe friends are people who feel your heart. You can share your secrets, cry, or laugh with them. Friends don't judge you or make you change. What do you think? Do you agree?" Sana asked Kevin.

"Good enough to tell you what I am looking for. But give me some time. I promise I won't take that long," Kevin giggled.

"I will wait. And you never know I might already know about what you're looking for," Sana giggled. "I want to know more about you, Kevin. Where are you from? Why are you here? I am sure for something more than just antiques."

Kevin smiled, but the question bothered him. He felt connected to Sana, but starting a relationship on a false narrative was no less than a crime. Kevin told himself that if you can't answer the truth, the best you can do is to dodge the question.

"I don't have any secret, Sana. I am a simple man who is a tourist in Mussoorie," Kevin smiled.

"Tourists don't come to Mussoorie to search for something important," Sana retorted.

She took a deep breath.

"It's okay if you want to keep it to yourself. I am here as your guide as promised."

"Sana, I am blessed to have you in my life. I want you to be my guide or friend, whatever you want. But stay with me. Please!" Kevin begged.

"Don't you think it's a bit selfish on your part? You want me to be with you as a friend or guide but won't tell me about yourself."

Sana was uncomfortable.

"It's hard to get a friend like you, Sana, and I don't want to lose you. Unfortunately, I am here for a reason that I cannot talk about right now. Sorry that I lied to you that I am a tourist, but I promise I will tell you everything one day when the time is right. Till that time, will you be my friend?"

"Friends don't have secrets between them. Treat me as your guide until you feel you can trust me. Until then, let's find what you are looking for."

Kevin and Sana looked at each other for a brief moment before Sana left. In those microseconds, their eyes told them what they wanted from each other was truth, trust, care, and, if possible a little love.

After Sana left, Kevin dialled a number in Kolkata in frustration.

"It's difficult for me. How can you think I can find that box in this big town? It is impossible."

"Do you have a choice? Either you find it or die. Brush up the searching skills that you acquired during your stay in Kolkata."

"It's not easy. And it is not safe too. Mussoorie has recently seen a mysterious death," Kevin said in a worried tone.

"Mysterious, fascinating. Enlighten me."

"There is news that someone was killed in Mussoorie with Chinese poison. God knows what's happening."

"Chinese poison?" Bijoy sounded worried.

"What happened?" Kevin was surprised by his reaction.

"Kevin, get me as many details you can about it by tomorrow. I need every minute detail. And keep your eyes open. It is the calm before the storm," Bijoy said and put down the phone.

***

Sana never felt the need to know someone so much. Kevin's acceptance that he was not in Mussoorie as a tourist was the approval of the lie that he told Sana. Sana wondered how the friendship, which started with a lie, could be trusted.

Baffled and worried, she reached home.

"Are you okay? You are looking worried." Sana's father switched off the TV and looked at her.

"Papa, what would you say about a friendship that started with a lie? Can it be trusted in the long run?" Sana asked.

"If someone lies to protect the friendship, then yes," her father replied. "Sometimes lies do not end the relationship, but the truth does," he added.

After a brief moment, he frowned and continued, "So, ask him why did he lie to you? If the answer is good enough to be trusted, then accept it. Otherwise move on."

Sana remembered that Kevin did say he wanted to protect her, which she now thought was an acceptable reason to give him a second chance to be trusted.

***

Kevin was puzzled by Bijoy's reaction to the news. He asked himself, *Why does he want to know more about this murder?*

Kevin decided to take a break and do something different to take his mind off all the worries. And then he remembered that it had been a long time since he met Alisha in college impersonating Rajat.

Kevin went to the room and stood in front of the mirror.

He slowly pulled off the band-aid on his forehead. The cut was gone, and the wound had healed without leaving a visible scar. He looked at it and gave a sarcastic smile, pulled out another, and stuck it at the same spot, to make Alisha believe that he was Rajat.

Kevin went to the college and went straight into the lab where Alisha was teaching. Alisha looked at Kevin from inside the lab and smiled at him. The band-aid had worked.

While waiting for Alisha at the lab, Kevin WhatsApped Rajat.

I am in MJK; where are you, pal?

Rajat looked at that message and felt annoyed. What was Kevin doing at MJK? He didn't need to go now. The litmus test had been done days ago.

Rajat responded to Kevin:

Kevin, don't meet Alisha. I want to sort out all of this with her. I will tell her the truth. Can we meet this evening? But for now, leave the college and wait for me at the hotel.

Kevin was surprised at the text from Rajat, but since Alisha had seen Kevin at the lab, he decided to meet her.

He responded that he would meet him in his room around six in the evening.

After a few minutes, Alisha walked out of the lab. They headed to the canteen.

"If I may ask you, can you protect the life of a person who is supposed to die soon? Can you do that legally?" Alisha asked Kevin after a while.

"That's an exciting question, but unfortunately, I will have to disappoint you. Firstly, I am a civil lawyer, so the case you are suggesting is for a criminal lawyer. Secondly, foremost, the lawyer's work will begin after someone dies, not when that individual is alive. But out of curiosity, why are you asking this?"

Alisha replied.

"I know someone who may be going to die soon. And I want to protect him at any cost."

Kevin wanted details, but Alisha did not say anything more. She thought she might Rajat in to more trouble if she took a legal path. So she decided to handle it by herself. In any case, Rajat was there to help her.

Searching for the box was becoming difficult for Kevin. He knew even if he ran away from Mussoorie without finding the box, Bijoy would get him out any rabbit hole he was hiding in. That thought bought forehead furrows, and Kevin went into deep thought for a brief moment.

Alisha saw the sudden change on Kevin's face and asked,

"What happened? You seem lost?"

Kevin snapped out of his thoughts.

"Nothing, sometimes work keeps me busy all the time. However, I am searching for something, and it looks like I will not be able to find it in this lifetime."

"What is it?" Alisha asked.

Kevin smiled and thought about Alisha's condition. She does not remember the faces she sees. So Kevin could show the Agha Netra to her and take a chance. But he forgot that Alisha only forgot faces, not the pictures.

"It's an antique box," Kevin said and pulled out the picture of the Agha Netra.

"Have you seen this before?"

Alisha was shocked to see the image and said, "Yes."

Kevin got a jolt when he heard her. His heart began to race.

"Are you sure you've seen this?"

Alisha nodded her head again.

"Yes, in my dream."

Kevin smiled and shook his head.

"Thanks. You just gave me a shock when you said that you had seen it."

Alisha looked at Kevin with tearful eyes.

"My dreams always come true, Rajat."

Kevin chuckled thinking she was joking.

"I hope this one comes true. And do let me know once you find it."

Another part of Kolkata

The Chinese triad, Bijoy's worst fear, was almost knocking on the door. Even if Bijoy knew the Agha Netra was in Mussoorie, they could lose it to the most unwanted guest – the triad. Sick with worry, Bijoy dialled a number and spoke in a low voice.

"You are right; the Agha Netra is in Mussoorie. I am not saying this because we've found it, but it looks like the Chinese have arrived in Mussoorie. They must be there for a reason. What else could it be other than the Agha Netra. Arinjay has shattered our trust. I can't believe that he was one among us!"

"Leave that, Bijoy, Arinjay is the past. But are you sure the Agha Netra is in Mussoorie?" the old husky voice on the other side of the phone asked.

"I am still awaiting more details. But if it turns out to be true, we need to move fast," Bijoy said.

"It is difficult to gather all the nine so soon."

He paused and continued, "Sorry, eight. But we do not have a choice. So let me ask them to be ready if the time comes."

The protectors did not have enough strength to stand against the Chinese triad. The Agha Netra was lost almost a century back and the rituals of all nine never took place. They remained connected with evolving communication, but today the eight were a pack of blunt knives.

To protect the Agha Netra, they needed young blood, which they could not find. They required a new generation whom they could trust.

***

The farther Rajat wanted to stay away from the Agha Netra, the closer it got to him. Now every day, it felt like it was somewhere close, especially after the death of Joy, and later when Alisha said she already knew about the box. Rajat started to think that this treasure was surely cursed. And finding it was as good as asking for trouble.

He reached the hotel and tiptoed past the reception, hiding from Sana. He swiftly went upstairs to Kevin's room.

He looked at Kevin and pointed to his forehead.

"Hasn't that healed?"

Kevin smiled and removed the band-aid.

"Indeed, yes, as if nothing happened."

"Probably, it is indicating to us that it's time to end the game we're playing with Alisha," Rajat was prompt to respond.

"You are right; it's not right to play with someone's emotions, especially when her condition is being mocked."

Kevin took a deep breath.

"But I will have to disappoint you, Rajat. I have to stay here for a few more days. So, I am not going to remove this soon."

Kevin picked up the band-aid and stuck it back.

"I am confused."

"I want this pretense of me being you to continue for a few more days."

"What does that mean? Do you think this is some kind of joke? You want to stay here and fool Alisha for fun now?"

Rajat was frustrated.

"See, Rajat, you put me up to this job, and I agreed to do it. So now I want an extension before I quit; what's the harm in it?" Kevin chuckled.

"Harm? You are playing with her emotions, Kevin. I am not sure how bad the damage is already," Rajat replied in a loud voice.

"And what about the litmus test? Is it over, Rajat? A litmus test on human feelings," Kevin chuckled and continued.

"Brother, only for a few days more. Then you go your way, I go mine."

Rajat wondered if he was indeed talking to Kevin. *Who was he? What happened to Kevin? Why was he behaving this way?*

Slowly things were getting out of control for Rajat. He wondered if it was the curse of the Agha Netra.

"Why do you sound so different, Kevin? Why are you here?" Rajat asked quietly.

"I came here to meet you, Rajat. It's just that I want to stay here a bit longer." Kevin smiled.

"It's not that simple, and I will find it out," Rajat paused.

"Anyway, I will let Alisha know the truth," he said in a determined tone.

"Rajat, see, there is something that I can't tell you right now. Give me a few days, and I will tell you all about it," Kevin said in a shallow voice.

"I don't understand what you mean. But I won't allow you, Kevin, to betray someone. Alisha has a problem, and I cannot play with her condition," Rajat said and left the room.

While leaving the hotel, Sana saw Rajat. She went over to him.

"Hey, Rajat. How are you? No band-aid. Your wound? Well, it looks okay."

Rajat looked at Sana.

"That was not a band-aid, Sana, it was a sign of betrayal. It's time to tell the truth and hurt someone. But I promise I will be the only one who will heal the pain with care and trust, and if she will accept, then with immense love."

Sana was awestruck by what Rajat said. That response indicated that Rajat had done something wrong, and he was guilty of it. Sana sincerely hoped that Alisha wasn't involved in whatever it was.

***

Things were never quite simple in Alisha's life. At every moment, she was at crossroads, not able to decide which choice to make or road to take. Now Kevin and Rajat were both looking for the box. Then who would die? Finding the truth is always thorny, and the road leading to it is not that easy either. Alisha then decided to look for the box by herself. It would save someone's life – either Rajat's or Kevin's. This way, she didn't have to worry. In the end it would be her bloody hands holding the box. Now it was time to get hold of it. Since both the men were still in Mussoorie, it meant that it was still in the town.

Alisha's mother was worried about her condition. Every day, Alisha looked more and more disturbed. She decided it was better to seek medical advice from a doctor. But since her face blindness had been detected, the doctor had given up on medical treatment. They said there were no medicines that could help. So, the only other option was spirituality as alternative medicine.

Finding the box by herself was a conscious decision taken by Alisha and she decided to tell her mother about it. When Alisha's mother heard of her decision, she became desperate for some spiritual help. Initially, her mother resisted and asked Alisha to forget about it all, but Alisha was adamant this time.

"I couldn't save two people, Ma. This time I have a chance. I have hope so let me try at least."

"In that case, Alisha, I will not stop you, but you will have to promise me that you must listen to whatever I say without any argument," her mother held Alisha's hand and pleaded. Alisha agreed.

Chapter 14

Let the Search Begin

Kevin remembered the instruction from Bijoy to inquire about the death from Chinese poison. It's hard to hide your identity if you show interest in a police investigation case. He was reluctant to go to the police station and ask for details about the murder. As a law graduate, he knew it wouldn't be easy for anyone to frame him; however, some questions did worry him. First and foremost, for the police anyone can be a suspect until the culprit is found. In any case, he didn't have a choice. So the only answer to his problem was to ask the police what had exactly happened. Finally, he managed to grease a few hands with few hundred-rupee notes. He spoke to a couple of constables and got the information he wanted. The police suspected the culprit was someone who looked Chinese or Nepalese.

Kevin called Bijoy and told him what he had learned about the case.

"I spoke to the police, and they suspect a Chinese or Nepalese national might be behind this murder. They are not ruling out other possibilities, but evidence indicates it's an outsider, not an Indian. Now, why did he do it? That reason is unknown."

Bijoy suspected that the Chinese triad had already stepped into Mussoorie. He knew it was time to gear up and protect the Agha Netra from the triad with whatever strength they had. The biggest question was how would he protect something when he didn't know its whereabouts. The Agha Netra was yet to be found. But the hunters were already sniffing in the right spot.

It was time for all eight to gather again after a long time. And this time, their main challenge was first, to find the Agha Netra, and then to protect it.

Arrival of the eight in Mussoorie

Bijoy wanted to keep the tradition of gathering at the Kali Ghat temple. So all eight gathered at night on the same day when Kevin had told Bijoy about the Chinese poison.

The bonfire was lit, and they all gathered close to the fire. Bijoy looked at them: they looked weak and worried. The Unknowns were aging fast, averagely aged between sixty and seventy years. It was not a good sign, and they needed to hand over the Agha Netra to the next generation as soon as possible.

One of the reasons they were so close to the fire was to keep them warm, rather than take the oath around the fire to save the Agha Netra.

One shaking voice asked Bijoy, "It is a shame that we are not able to protect it. How will we be able to find it now, Bijoy? Look at us."

Bijoy looked at the burning fire, and his eyes lit up its reflection.

"The Agha Netra was handed over to us with faith. To the nine protectors. To the Nine Unknowns. There was something within us, and that was the reason why we are here. Today we all have to look inside ourselves to find our greatness. We all are fighters, and life has kept us in a pit for a long time. We have to rise today and prove why we're great. Life will keep pulling us down." He paused, stood up, looked around at each one of them.

"Look, it will not be easy; you will get tired and you will be exhausted. You will feel lost in the battle. But we all have to remember one thing: as long as you never give up, you will win and find it. You will get the Agha Netra."

The other voice said, "Let this life have some meaning. Let us all live for a purpose and die for a reason. Let us all do it for the pride of being protectors."

This time the eight felt the real greatness in themselves, and they all understood one thing that day.

You must realize your potential the most when you are at the weakest or lowest point of your life.

The very next day they all left for Mussoorie. They were to meet a priest Bijoy knew in Mussoorie town.

***

Sana had a faint memory of her grandfather. She remembered her grandfather's forehead, which was covered with deep wrinkles, and his eyes pale like the dawn. Yet, even at the age of eighty, his eyesight was as strong as his willpower to stand straight without a walking stick. Indeed, life had left a deep imprint on his face.

She remembered calling him 'Baba' while her grandfather called her 'Laddu'. At that age, she didn't know what her Baba used to be when he was young. But he always used to tell a story of the demigod and how he fought the enemies of our family. His story was so dramatic that Sana would always imagine it in her dreams. There used to be a puzzle that demigods would give to the protagonist. Once the puzzle was solved, the protagonist would get closer to what he was hunting for.

Sana disliked the part where the hero went through pain to solve the puzzle in the story. But she eagerly waited for the moment when the hero would meet the princess in the story. Or sometimes, the protagonist became the hero of his village when he saved the poor.

Soon after, when Baba left the world, little Sana used to sleep on the same bed, waiting for her Baba to return one day and tell her the story.

Not often did she remember Baba, but that day she felt a deep sense of void. Sana reached out to the book where her father kept the letter that Baba had written. The letter was a collection of the words written cryptically. People told her that Baba had lost his senses when he was on his deathbed, so he wrote something without any meaning.

But Sana never believed that. Instead, she opened the letter and decided to decipher it, wondering if Baba might have left a puzzle for her to solve.

***

The Golden Gate Hotel was a relatively less busy dwelling for travellers which left Sana with some time to read and understand Baba's letter while at work.

The cafe was the best place to decipher the cryptic clues and determine what each word meant.

"Is someone trying hard to figure out a secret map?" Kevin smiled as he came up to Sana's table.

"It is not that easy, Kevin. Clues are sometimes written in such a way that they'll send you on a wild goose's chase," Sana replied.

"Cryptic, or is it cynical?" Kevin pulled up a chair and sat in front of Sana.

"Cryptic, that is right. Optimistic is another word."

Sana looked at Kevin.

"Why are you here? Do you need a guide again?"

Kevin knew that he was being selfish by not revealing why he was in Mussoorie. And that kept him away from being Sana's friend.

In life, you may meet a person who takes away your worries in the blink of an eye. One with whom you feel an invisible connection. Just by watching the person smile. Kevin felt the same for Sana but he felt he was losing her at every meeting.

"Can that guide find me a friend?"

Sana looked at him.

"Friends are like diamonds; no one can guide you to find that bling," she replied.

Kevin smirked.

Sana thought that it would be fair to show Kevin the letter. She remembered Kevin talking about examples of decoding messages, images, and text. To ensure that Kevin would take the work of interpreting the letter seriously, she decided to tell him that it belonged to Baba.

"I remembered you spoke to me about cryptic and subliminal messages. How good are you at decrypting something?"

"If it's a test of my knowledge, I would not like to take it and fail. But if you need a helping hand, then I can try," he said.

"A friend in need is a friend indeed," Sana said. She drew her chair closer to his and gave it to him.

She warned Kevin that he shouldn't joke about it if he could not figure out what it meant. The letter was close to her heart.

As Kevin gingerly unfolded the yellowed parchment, the faint scent of history wafted through the air. The letter, weathered by time, held secrets of a bygone era. These words started to dance in front of Kevin. Its delicate script sprang across the page, enticing him to decipher its hidden message.

Lines and words that seemed simple at first glance carried a deeper meaning. A reference to 'symbols' and 'the old deodar tree' sparked a sense of adventure. He asked himself, *could this be a map leading to a forgotten treasure or a long-lost secret?*

The letter mentioned an old deodar tree that stood majestically in a forgotten corner of Mussoorie. Beneath its gnarled roots lay a small tarnished box.

What Kevin was about to see next in the letter would undoubtedly make him more worried than before. When he saw the sign of the eye, his smile disappeared like dancing water droplets evaporating from a hot pan.

Kevin looked at the letter closely, with his eyes staring and scanning at each word as if they meant something on their own. He frowned at a few words and worried about a few. His darting eyes and the wrinkles on his forehead were enough signs to comfort Sana that Kevin was serious about the letter and its contents.

Kevin exhaled a deep breath, holding the letter and looked at Sana.

"This letter is about something hidden somewhere. I have yet to understand it completely. But some words are very uniquely placed. Like at instance, it says a group of trees in the jungle will tell you the sign. Now, see Sana, a jungle is full of trees, so what does a group of trees in the jungle mean? At one glance, you feel that it is written by someone who lost his senses while writing it, but if you look closer, think what a hidden sign in a jungle could be. Something which is in front of you but you can't see easily. Like a group of trees arranged in a particular way."

Sana was baffled, but she was happy to know that the letter had some meaning.

"I need some time to decipher this letter. And if you want to discover the hidden thing in the letter, I could be your guide."

Sana pursed up her lips, closed her eyes, and remained silent for a few minutes.

"Let's do a trade-off. I will allow you to be my help, but before that, answer me—" Sana looked at Kevin.

Kevin cut her short.

"What am I doing in Mussoorie?" he sighed.

Sana smiled.

In the next ten minutes, Kevin explained to Sana why he was in Mussoorie. Kevin did it to win Sana's trust. But unknowingly, he was killing two birds with one stone. One was to win Sana's trust, and the other might lead him to the object in the letter, which he was sure was none other than the Agha Netra. The only part which he hid from Sana was that he knew Rajat and that Alisha thought he was Rajat.

***

Alisha was clueless about looking for the blood-drenched box. She had no idea where to even start. One thought that kept coming into her mind was if she could only see the dream again in which she had seen the hand holding the box, she could perhaps get some clues. Now the big question was how to dream about something that you want. To find an answer, she Googled a few searches on 'How to dream about what you want'. A suggestion was to keep the picture of the thing next to your bed and look at it before you sleep. She found this to be an easy method, so she quickly doodled the image she saw in her dreams and kept it near her bed.

The first night, it didn't work.

The next day morning, her mother came into the room and saw that piece of paper with an image of the Agha Netra kept on the bedside table. She frowned and woke up Alisha.

"What is this?" her mother asked.

Alisha quickly took the paper from her mother's hand and folded it.

"It's like an experiment. If you want to dream about something, keep it at your bedside and you will see it in your dream."

Alisha looked at her mother earnestly.

"I want to dream about it, Ma. I want to find a clue from it."

"Is it the same box?" her mother asked worryingly.

"Yes, it is."

"I always wanted to escape these dreadful dreams, but today I want to chase them. Maybe I can save someone's life this time."

Alisha's mother looked at her in surprise. Alisha had always wanted to escape from her dreams, but now she was doing the opposite. She feared it would become a vicious circle with Alisha's condition. Her face blindness was enough trouble as it is. And now coupled with the dreams, she would only worsen. She knew someone in town who could help.

The next day, Alisha followed the same routine. That night, she found herself running through a jungle of deodar trees. Relentless and puffed, her eyes were searching for something. Finally, after running for a few more minutes, she saw a small hut. It stood out in the middle of the deep jungle. Alisha was mesmerized. She walked through the door.

It was dark inside. She waited for a minute and moved. And then she saw it again. From the dark appeared a pair of hands, drenched in blood, holding a box.

Alisha woke up with a start and sat up on the bed. She looked at the clock. It was three in the morning – the same time she'd been waking up after the dreams that came true. She swiftly took a pen and paper and jotted down the scene she had seen.

That night the experiment had worked. Alisha got two clues – the deodar forest and a hut. But a hut in a deodar forest was a very common sight, especially in and around Mussoorie. It could be anywhere, but mostly where snowfall occurs.

That day in the MJK college canteen, as she tried to zero in on the location, someone tapped her table. She looked up at with narrowed eyes.

It was Rajat who was impersonating Kevin. The guy smiled.

"Let me help you. It's me, Kevin," he said as he pulled up a chair.

"Hmm…" Alisha said lost in deep thoughts.

"Is that normal or I should be surprised?" he asked her.

She swiftly looked at the bracelet in his hand, which confirmed that he was Kevin.

"I was thinking about a location where you can find deodar trees. Do you know any such place?" Alisha was prompt in asking.

"It's quite common near Mussoorie. There are a lot of places in the outskirts," Rajat replied, leaning back on the chair.

"May I ask why?"

"See Kevin, I want to save someone's life. God has given me a chance, and I don't want to lose it. So if I reach the box before it reaches you or Rajat, I can save someone."

"Rajat? Who is he? Does he also know about the box?"

"Rajat is a lawyer here working for a case for the college. He told me one day that he's also looking for the box with the eye on it."

Rajat was shocked. Why was Kevin also looking for the box? What did he have anything to do with it? At the same time, it dawned on him why Kevin was so reluctant to leave town. Or stop contact with Alisha.

He got up immediately from the chair when he understood this.

"What happened, Kevin? You look worried."

"Yes, I am. If you get to it first, Alisha, that hand could be yours," he said grimly.

Alisha smiled.

"That would be even better. I will manage to save someone. If I—"

Kevin quickly covered Alisha's mouth gently with his palm.

"I will not let that happen, Alisha," he paused and said. "From now on, I will be by your side in your search for that box. And I promise that hand drenched in blood will be mine."

Alisha was frozen. It was the first time a boy had touched her.

***

Alisha's mother decided to meet the Saint Anityo to understand what was going on in Alisha's life. Would her dreadful dreams end in this lifetime.? Would her face blindness be cured? Would she live a normal life?

There were a thousand questions that Alisha's mother wanted to ask, but the worry was, what if even the saint did not have any answer to these? Or if there was something even worse to come?

Alisha's mother reached the house near the Santura Devi Temple. The outer walls of the house were coloured white. The top of the house had a triangular saffron flag flurrying in the wind. There were shoes and flip-flops at the doorstep, indicating there were people inside. Yet, even with so many people inside the house, the quietness made the place feel like a monastery. As soon as Alisha's mother entered the room, she saw a man in his late sixties. He was short with pale skin and a long clean-shaven face. He was sitting cross-legged with his eyes closed in Buddha's lotus position. The room was so quiet that she could only hear her own footsteps.

Everyone around Saint Anityo was still looking at him, mesmerized by his aura, and god-like stature.

After a few minutes, Saint Anityo opened his eyes, looked at Alisha's mother, and smiled. She fumbled, folded her hands, and bowed.

"I know why you are here, Kamla. Come and sit in front of me," his soft-spoken voice instructed Alisha's mother to walk towards him and sit.

"Shiva himself blesses your daughter. Why are you worrying about her?"

Kamla was surprised, but it came with relief that without saying a word, the saint knew her worries already. She was in the right place.

"She has suffered a lot; I can't see her in more pain as a mother."

Saint Anityo smiled.

"Suffering is necessary for life when you are born for a cause or a purpose. She will soon realize the purpose of her dreams. She needs your support at this time."

The response was blended with true but unconvincing words. The truth because Saint Anityo was right about Alisha's dreams and unconvincing because how could someone be blessed with such dreadful dreams? Kamla wanted to know more about Alisha's life but she thought she got all the answers in the two sentences. While Kamla was baffled about whether to stay or leave, suddenly the loud stomping of feet broke the silence. Eight men burst into the room.

Saint Anityo looked at them with a smile, pointed his hand in one direction.

"Feel free to use the room and relax. I will join you there."

The eight men followed each other and went inside the room across the hall.

Kamla stood up and started to walk out of the room.

"Kamla, Alisha needs you the most. When you had come earlier, I told you to stay with her. I will say the same words now," he said in a calm voice.

Kamla stopped and turned around.

"She dreams about the people who are going to die. When it started, she wanted to get away from these dreams. But now she is trying to stop these deaths by returning to the same dream. It is taking over her life."

"It is all because Shiva wanted to serve a purpose through her dreams," the saint replied.

"I pray you are right. The eye in her dreams could be Shiva's eye. Though I hope Shiva doesn't open his third eye on her," saying that Kamla walked out, wiping her tears.

***

Alisha's dreams were a surprise. He thought Kamla had come because of Alisha's face blindness. But when he learned that Alisha could see the future of a person who would die soon, he realized how powerful she was.

Almost an hour after Kamla left, Saint Anityo stopped his interaction with devotees. He stepped into the room where the eight men were waiting for him. They looked tired. A few were already dozing off on the sofa.

"It must have been a tiring journey from Kolkata. Only you are defying your age, Bijoy," he said addressing the old man.

"My purpose in my life is not letting me grow older," Bijoy replied and shrugged.

Bijoy's purpose in Mussoorie was secret to the Saint, and he too didn't want to ask Bijoy more about his visit. Finally, Bijoy told Saint Anityo that he wanted to stay in Mussoorie for a few days.

"You are most welcome, Bijoy. I hope your purpose for visiting Mussoorie is met with success. In case you need some help spiritually, I am here," Saint Anityo assured him.

The first thing Bijoy decided to do was meet his friend, Kevin. He dialled Kevin's number.

"I am here in the Queen of Hills and hope you will welcome me," he said.

Kevin, on another side, were stung by those words. He replied in a shaking voice,

"What are you doing here?"

"The Agha Netra is in danger," he said with a smirk. "And you too!" he added before hanging up.

***

Rajat was fuming when he found out that Kevin was also searching for the box, and that had he had not mentioned it to him. But Rajat had another important question that worried him. Why was Kevin after that box? Kevin was deceiving Alisha and hiding the truth from Rajat as well. What was going on?

After pondering about it, he decided to ask Sana for help.

That evening he reached the Golden Gate Hotel and parked his bike on the other side of the road. He started to walk towards the hotel when he suddenly saw a few well-built men accosting Kevin into a van. As the scene unfolded in front of him, Rajat understood there was something fishy going on. He ran back to his bike and began to trail the van.

After driving a few metres ahead, a scooter stopped in front of him.

"Hello Rajat, what are you doing here?"

It was Sana.

Rajat looked at Sana and then saw the van accelerate and leave the scene.

"I need to talk to you. Shall we sit in the cafe?" Rajat sighed and told Sana.

Rajat and Sana walked into the cafe and sat across a table. Rajat put his hands on the table and shook his head in disappointment. He didn't know where to begin and how much to reveal. Amidst his dilemma, his thoughts returned to Kevin. *What was happening with Kevin? Who were the men who took Kevin?*

Sana waited for a few minutes, squinted her eyes, and said, "If I could only hear what thoughts are gushing in your mind. Unfortunately, I am not a mind-reader. So, a few words will help," she said and grinned.

Rajat looked up at her and replied, "I should say thank God that we can't read people's minds. Else, the relationship would not have lasted long. People think something else, speak something else, and do something else. Here trust is at a stage just before a broken heart or a broken relationship."

Sana frowned. "Seems like a serious issue. What happened? You don't look like you today."

"You know Kevin?" Rajat asked.

"Yes, I know," Sana replied.

"We have known each other since college days," Rajat paused for Sana's reaction.

Sana replied worryingly, "But he never said anything about you, why?"

"Did he tell you the reason for his visit to Mussoorie?" Rajat asked.

"Yes, he is here in search of a century-old box. It feels like a treasure hunt for him," she replied.

Rajat was surprised. He told had told Sana but had hidden it from him.

"I need your help, Sana. I feel that Kevin is in trouble. If you see anything suspicious, would you let me know?" Rajat said. "I know him very well; even if he is trouble, he won't tell me about it. So, I need you to tell me about him. Will you help?" he added.

Sana was completely baffled. *What was going on?* But momentarily she said, "Okay."

***

In the ashram, Saint Anityo was busy meeting devotees, meditating, and reading spiritual books about the Buddha. In the last few years, he had developed an interest in knowing how the Buddha understood and addressed people's problems. Saint Anityo's past was unknown to many people in Mussoorie. He had come to the hills around ten years back, and since then, he had been meeting devotees who had gradually grown in large numbers. Saint Anityo was never interested in hosting any assembly to preach or a procession. He lived a slow life quietly in his ashram, away from the madding crowd.

While he was busy reading about the Buddha, few men walked into his ashram. They were acquaintances, but he remembered the faces he had seen the first time.

One of them walked towards Saint Anityo.

"You know our purpose, Saint Anityo. I was told that you would be of some help. But it looks like you are busy listing the pain of others, and not ours."

Saint Anityo realized who they were but remained calm.

"What information did you get from the librarian?

"He spilled out everything he knew. Unfortunately, we had to quieten him because he threatened us with police action."

That response discomforted Saint Anityo. He leaned forward and replied in a low but angry voice.

"Joy was one of my devotees. I gave you his address only for you to get information about the box. But you guys are inhuman."

He pointed at his book and continued,

"In *Dhammapada,* the Buddha says, that an action, even if it benefits oneself, cannot be considered a good action if it causes physical and mental pain to another being," Saint Anityo stated and leaned back.

The man smiled.

"Doesn't the same apply to you, Anityo? Please don't lecture us about killing someone. You are a call away from landing in prison."

After a brief pause, he continued in a calm voice.

"Anyway, we just came here to remind you that it is still to be found. While you speak to these innocent devotees, keep your ears open. And get your network working to locate it."

He tapped Saint Anityo's shoulder and walked out of the room.

As they left, Saint Anityo remembered his horrific past, which made him numb after the conversation.

Chapter 15

Spill the Beans – What was in a Name?

Kevin knew that he should be worried since Bijoy was in town. Sitting in the van he decided that he would let Bijoy know about Alisha and Sana in case things got out of control. And they did. As soon as the van stopped, Bijoy and the two bodyguards pulled Kevin out of the van and smashed his face with punches.

The first blow was enough for Kevin to spill out all the information he had, but he remained calm. The second bodyguard came from behind and punched him in the back. This blow got Kevin speaking. He held up both his hands.

"Wait, Wait! I have something to share!"

Bijoy came up to him and said in a commanding voice, "Spit it out!"

Kevin was as clear as he could as he explained about Alisha and Sana. Bijoy, after listening to Kevin, thought that Sana's cryptic letter probably contained the closest lead to the Agha Netra's location. And Alisha's dream was like a map with map-counters to reach the place.

He gave him two days to get the letter from Sana and give it to him. Kevin had no choice. While returning to the town, the van dropped Kevin near the MJK college gate.

After the van left, Kevin stood there for a while looking at the van go out of his sight. He was in deep pain, barely able stand on his feet. Finally, he realized how he had betrayed both Sana and Alisha. He felt overwhelmed and needed to speak to someone. He wanted to get it off his chest. At that moment he saw Alisha coming out of the college gate on her scooter.

He rushed towards her.

"Hey, how are you? I am Kevin."

Alisha looked at that tangled hair, bruised face and hand without the bracelet. She was confused and decided to walk away.

Kevin knew about the bandage.

"I have no bandages on my face. The wound has healed."

For Alisha, every face had a passcode and to unlock Rajat's face, it was a bandage for Rajat. Just as it was the bracelet for Kevin's face. If she didn't get that passcode the face remained hidden.

Alisha turned back.

"The Kevin I know never had a bracelet. Who are you? Do I know you?"

Kevin walked up to her.

"I am not Rajat. I am Kevin."

Alisha was baffled and worried. How did the guy know both the names? She knew people often made fun of her condition, but it hurt the most when someone misused trust and used it to take advantage of her.

Kevin asked Alisha if she could listen to him for a few minutes so that he could explain everything.

"Alisha, I have to tell you something that you should know," Kevin continued while cleaning his face with his shirt.

"What you saw in your dream about that box has got many lives on line. And I am one of them. I am Kevin who had the bandage on his forehead. Probably that's the only sign that identifies me. And I need help."

Alisha was lost. But what she could gather was that her face blindness was not a secret anymore.

"Then Rajat? And what's in that box?"

"Rajat is my friend, and we exchanged our identities for some reason; that you don't want to know. And what's in that box is a mystery to each one of us. See, I can help Rajat but you have to tell me what else you know about that box," Kevin said in a serious tone.

Alisha was miffed. She felt the people she trusted were the ones who were with her for a selfish reason. She was thinking of saving a life, but people around her were chasing death in search of that box.

"Why I should tell you Kevin? I am losing faith in myself by trusting others. I don't know whether it is you or Rajat who is telling me the truth. I better leave the box to its fate."

Alisha was shaken.

"You don't have an option other than trusting me, Alisha. Rajat's life could be in danger if he reaches that box first. It could be me or Rajat. I want him to live. I want him to be safe," Kevin pleaded.

Alisha got up.

"The last thing I saw about it was a jungle of deodar trees and a small temple. I don't know if it is some place near Mussoorie or elsewhere. And whoever you are Kevin or Rajat, I have only one mission. That is to save someone's life. You guys have broken my trust by confusing me and taking advantage of my condition. However, I feel the cost of saving a life is higher than broken trust," she said angrily.

"I don't want to meet either of you. Thanks for being honest when you found yourself in danger. How selfish. And telling me the truth was for yourself, not for me. Now I realize that being face blind is god's gift so that I don't remember faces of dodgers and can stay away from being hurt."

Alisha walked away, saddened, broken and hurt.

***

Alisha reached home, tired, quiet, and helpless. She felt that there was no cure for her worries. After her father had left the world, problems followed her one after another. And she was becoming weaker and weaker with each passing day. But the most painful was to keep these worries hidden from her mother. She knew her mother had faced enough troubles in her life. Her mother watched her as she went to her room. She knew that she was riddled with worry. As Saint Anityo had told Kamla to stay with Alisha, she decided that listening and talking to her might be the only way to help her. She would sit down with her later.

Chapter 16

A Throne to Conquer

Saint Anityo was anxious. He turned to his faith and sought solace in prayer, finding comfort in his belief that a higher power was in control. He felt a sense of surrender, trusting in divine guidance to navigate through his worries and find inner peace. He almost forgot his reason for being in Mussoorie. Saint Anityo's calm demeanour and unwavering faith, while inspiring others to embrace serenity and seek spiritual refuge in times of anxiety, was wavering.

That evening he went near the edge of the hill and felt a sense of tranquillity wash over him as the gentle breeze whispered serenely through the surrounding trees. He sat in a meditation posture where he crossed his legs, placing each foot on the opposite thigh, like Buddha, symbolizing stability and being grounded, while promoting an upright posture conducive to deep concentration and inner stillness.

After a few minutes into the mediation, he felt someone walk near him and sit beside him. The footsteps broke his meditation like someone had thrown a pebble into calm and still water. He gently opened his eyes and saw a girl; at first glance it looked like she was from China, but he also could see a blend of Indian features.

She looked at Saint Anityo with calm eyes and smiled. Anityo was mesmerized; he remained quiet, looking at her.

"I am Arini from Xiamen," she said.

Arini was a Chinese-Indian mix girl, a fusion of two rich cultures, blending the grace and elegance of Chinese heritage with the vibrant colours and diverse traditions of India, creating a unique and captivating identity that celebrated the best of both worlds.

Arini possessed a graceful presence, standing tall at about five feet five inches, with a slender graceful frame, radiating an aura of elegance and charm.

She was beautiful.

"How can I help you, Arini?" Saint Anityo asked softly.

"Help?" she smiled and continued, "That is one a thing you haven't done since the last ten years, Anityo! Looks like while in search of solace, you've forgotten the reason why you came to Mussoorie in the first place."

The words sent chills down his spine. It didn't take him much time to realize that he was meeting Arini, the powerful front runner to the throne of the Xiamen triad.

"I have to come down here as you have not done your job yet. I know that the Agha Netra is in Mussoorie, and those dogs from Kolkata are already sniffing here."

The calm voice gave way to a sharp tone cutting through the air, leaving an unsettling residue of tension. The soothing words suddenly turned into sharp daggers.

"My men have been looking for it for many years now. But they haven't even found a clue to its whereabouts. There was one guy who knew something about it, but he was killed. Are you sure it's here in Mussoorie?" Anityo asked, frowning.

"Joy was killed because he didn't like being questioned. He wanted to go to the police. Anityo, my grandfather had told me a story about a mysterious box. He thought I was a naïve adolescent girl. And I'd listen to the story like any other teenage girl. But he was mistaken. He was telling me all about the Agha Netra, its power, and the Nine Unknowns. He did not know that this submissive girl had the ambition to lead the most deadly triad one day. And for that, I need to take the Agha Netra back to Xiamen to prove my worth, where people are waiting to crown me queen as soon as I show them the Agha Netra," Arini said with an air of finality.

"Are you sure that your grandfather told you the true story of the Agha Netra?" Anityo asked.

"My grandfather…" Arini chuckled, "Arinjay Biswas can't be wrong. He was one of the Nine Unknowns who last held the Agha Netra in his hands."

The words hit Anityo like a bullet. He knew that Arinjay had betrayed the Nine Unknowns, and he was the only person who knew about the Agha Netra. And, Arini was the granddaughter of Arinjay, who had come to get the Agha Netra back.

One thing was clear from Arini was that Arinjay didn't betray the Nine Unknowns but kept the promises by hiding the Agha Netra from the world till it was found. But only time would tell how long it would remain hidden because now people were hunting for the treasure desperately at the right place.

After that brief meeting, Arini left Anityo at the hill more disturbed than before. She had come to Mussoorie to conquer the throne of Xiamen, but, unknowingly, she was in Mussoorie to prove Arinjay had been loyal to the Nine.

In that troubled state of mind, Anityo was unable to find any solution. He needed help to get a clue or find any lead. He started to think hard. Who else had talked about the eye or anything similar to the subject? The last person he knew was Kamla, who had come to find a solution for her daughter. It was shooting in the dark, but Anityo decided to get more information from Kamla about her daughter's dream and the eye.

Chapter 17

Kabandha, the Demon

Demons arise as complex beings, challenging the gods and testing the limits of human existence, reminding us of the intricate nature of our own inner battles.

Anityo called Kamla over. He asked her to sit in front of the Buddha, and meditate for a while. After a while Anityo asked her to listen to him carefully.

"Kamla, yesterday I thought a lot about Alisha and her condition. I was not able to find a solution for her. I'm worried that something could happen, and I will not be able to stop it," Saint Anityo said looking worried.

Kamla became anxious; those words added fuel to her worries about Alisha's condition. She remained quiet, looking at Saint Anityo. Anityo took a deep breath and exhaled.

"Have you heard about Kabandha Demon?" Anityo asked his face etched with worry. "Kabandha was a demon in the Ramayana. He was a monstrous demon with unique physical characteristics. He was a headless demon; his mouth was in his belly. He had one huge eye on his forehead, which was actually on his chest. That terrible demon wandered in the Dandaka forest.

"One day, Ram and Lakshman were wandering through the same forest and there they encountered the demon. His grotesque appearance made him a terrifying sight. As soon as Kabandha saw them, he caught them both. They had been searching for Sita after Ravan had kidnapped her.

"The demon caught Ram and Lakshman in his enormous arms. It was hard to escape from those mighty arms. As it was getting difficult to escape the demon, Rama and Lakshman took out a sword and cut his arm. Losing his arms, which were his strength, Kabandha was about to die. Seeing his death looming, the demon introduced himself to Ram and Lakshman. He said that he was a Gandharva, a most handsome man. But he had been cursed by a sage, Sthulashiras. This was because he used to scare and harass saints and humans. The only way Kabandha could reverse the curse was if Ram would cut his hand and cremate him after his death."

Saint Anityo stopped for a moment.

"I am worried the eye which Alisha is seeing in her dream could be that of the demon Kabandha. He has caught Alisha. To save Alisha, we need to find how Alisha is connected with that eye. We must find and kill that monster to relieve her from the curse."

Kamla knew something was wrong with that eye, but a curse on her princess? She would have never imagined it even in her dreams.

In a shaking voice, she asked, "What can we do about it, Saint Anityo? How can we save her?"

"First you tell me what do you know about Alisha's dream and the eye?" he asked her.

In the next few minutes, Kamla explained Alisha's dream and that mysterious box. As soon as Anityo heard about the box, he was startled but didn't let his expression give away anything. While talking and understanding more about Alisha, he asked Kamla to draw the box. The weird-looking abstract shapes and lines Kamla drew were familiar to Saint Anityo. He was looking at the Agha Netra. The box which everyone was looking for in Mussoorie. And now, Alisha's dream was the window through which he could reach the box.

Anityo picked up the paper and held it up in front of his eyes. He then looked at Kamla and said, "Look at this eye, Kamla; I am worried about how much trouble Alisha is in. She is in the grip of that demon; we need to find this box as soon as possible."

Kamla nodded her head. Anityo told Kamla that she should keep updating Anityo about Alisha's dreams and what she does. But he told Kamla to be cautious and make sure that Alisha wasn't aware of them.

"But what about the blood drenched hands?" Kamla stammered.

"Believe in Lord Ram. He will help us to cut those hands," Anityo said.

After Kamla left the ashram, Anityo picked up the landline phone and dialled a number.

"It's going to be serious and nasty. I think I know where is Agha Netra. You keep an eye on her. She is in Mussoorie. If she comes to know that I have the Agha Netra, then I will have to hand it over to her."

The man on the other side of the phone said, "That bitch. She is dreaming of conquering the throne. You get hold of that Agha Netra and I will protect you from being arrested."

Anityo thanked him and kept the receiver down.

***

In another part of Mussoorie, Rajat was desperate to reveal the truth to Alisha about himself and Kevin. He had waited for hours in the MJK canteen but she didn't turn up. He looked all around in the college but Alisha was nowhere to be found. He came back to the canteen and sat on a chair. Leaning backwards, he closed his eyes with one leg stretched out, blocking the path.

"Excuse me" a soft voice requested Rajat to move his leg. Rajat opened his eyes.

Alisha was standing in front of him in a red kurta and white pajamas. She radiated grace as she looked at Rajat. With a single glance, his heart skipped a beat as her eyes met his. In that split second, Rajat said to himself, *Is this how it feels... love at first sight?*

He slowly moved his leg and watched her sit down at a table nearby.

Alisha sat on the chair, staring randomly around the canteen. The face blindness had made her aloof from society, but still, she could not come to terms with the fact that people she trusted could break her heart so easily. Once the search was over, she decided to leave the place forever and move away to Delhi, in the hope that the new place would help her rewrite her destiny.

Rajat silently walked up to her and threw the wrist band on the table. The noise, bought Alisha back into the MJK canteen and she looked down at the table. Her anger returned as she lay eyes on the band.

"I am sorry!" Rajat said sheepishly.

"What should I call you – Rajat or Kevin?" Alisha lashed out.

The response shocked Rajat. He was surprised that Alisha knew about Kevin and himself.

Meanwhile, Alisha got up from her chair and started to walk out of the canteen. Rajat was adamant to tell her his side of the story. He grabbed Alisha hand and pulled her towards him. She came close to Rajat, very close.

"I will not let you go unless you listen to what I have to say," Rajat begged with soulful eyes.

Alisha looked into his eyes and relented.

Rajat explained everything to Alisha and confessed his idea of a litmus test. His words were filled with remorse as he looked into her eyes, seeking forgiveness.

Alisha, with crossed arms and a stern gaze, shook her head, unable to forgive him yet. Her heart was still guarded by the pain he had caused.

After listening to Rajat's story Alisha was still unable to accept his apology and believe that Rajat wouldn't do it again. She told Rajat that Kevin had met her and had told her about them conspiring to switch identities.

"Look Rajat, I will not be in a position to trust anyone so soon. I am hurt and broken. People say time heals everything, But I can tell you time doesn't heal. The truth is healing is the letting go of the attachment we have with people, situation and things.

"But most people take time to let go of this attachment. I want to find that box and save someone's life. Either yours or Kevin's, I don't know. On the path to find that mystery, I will walk alone," Alisha replied.

Rajat picked up the wrist band and wore it again.

"Whether you trust me or not, is not my problem. But in search of that box, I will be with you. I don't care about this MJK case anymore. I will do what my heart says," Rajat said in a determined tone. "That is, to be with you always," he added as he watched Alisha's retreating back.

These words reached Alisha as she was walking out of the canteen. She stopped briefly and then walked towards the gate.

***

Rajat bravely told Alisha how he felt, which broke his inner pain, set him free from suffering, and made him feel better inside. In the next few days, Rajat met with Alisha and with his sincere efforts he managed to pacify her up to a certain extent, that she agreed to let him help her.

Rajat had fallen in love with Alisha. It was just that he didn't want her to go, so he kept his feelings to himself. During the search for the box, Alisha told Rajat that she had also dreamt of a temple. And they should search for a temple which has a similar landscape around it. They decided to go into a nearby jungle to start the search.

Deodar trees in the woods grow in an uneven symmetrical pattern. If you're not careful, it's easy to lose your way from where you started. Rajat was following Alisha and kept watching every step. It was a random search, and they knew the success was not going to come easy. They were ready to fail, but not give up.

The race to locate the Agha Netra had started. Some pure hearts were searching to save someone's life, few to keep the century old promise while others wanted to use the Agha Netra as a trade-off to get the throne.

While all that was happening in Mussoorie, Sana was busy decoding the letter, while Kevin was trying to figure to how to escape from the clutches of Bijoy.

A bruised Kevin, with few faint scars on his face, was sitting in the cafe of the Golden Gate Hotel. Anyone could figure out that he had been ruthlessly beaten or had met with an accident.

In the hotel, work didn't keep Sana too busy. So, most of the time she was busy looking at the letter from her grandfather. Slowly she was drifting towards the thought that her grandfather may have indeed become senile, writing a letter which didn't make any sense to anyone.

Thinking about the letter she walked into the cafe. Soft music was playing in the cafe and almost empty hall was the apt place to try to understand what his grandfather wanted to say. As she glanced around, it was easy for her to spot Kevin in the hall, sitting in the corner staring out of the window, lost in his own thoughts.

She walked up to him.

"Why it is that you are always getting hurt? Do you always pick fights?" Sana chuckled.

Kevin looked at Sana, took a deep breath and again started looking out of the window.

"It's gift for all my sins and mistakes. I don't think I am going to come out of it soon."

He smiled and continued, "It will keep coming to me in tranches."

Sana felt there was something serious going on, so she chose to stay with him and listen. A friend in deed, now had a chance to be a friend in need.

"You can talk to me. I am all ears," Sana said sitting down.

To distract Kevin from his thoughts, she placed the letter in front of him.

"Let's work on it together." Sana smiled.

Kevin pulled the letter towards him.

"What you think about this letter, Sana?"

"Honestly Kevin, if I speak my mind, I'm starting to feel that my grandfather was not in his senses when he wrote it." Sana frowned.

Kevin chuckled.

"Listen to this:

> *Mystic blaze concealed, veiled and unseen, Weapons covert, shadows intervene, unveiling power where whispers convene."*

"I don't get it. Sounds cryptic, not aligned with any context," Sana replied.

"It's a masterstroke, Sana! Your grandfather is talking about weapons which he hides. Might be for the freedom struggle back then," Kevin said sitting up in excitement.

"And so, but it's not aligned to context. My grandfather was a Gandhian. Ahimsa was the path he always took," Sana replied.

"See at times, one might be inflicted with wounds of injustice. This can bring his calm mind to cease. An oppressed mind can choose violence to respond to injustice. He might not have used these weapons, but he definitely had them!"

"Now why did he have those weapons, whether he used them or not? How it is linked to what he is saying in that story? We need to closely read this letter and decode it. "

"We should visit some historical sites which were part of freedom struggle. Might be we can find a clue there," Sana said.

"No harm in looking around. So is this a friend in need for a deed!" Kevin smiled.

"Yes, he is, indeed," Sana chuckled.

Chapter 18

Believe in You

Bijoy was waiting for Kevin to hand over the letter which Sana's Baba had written. Other than that, he didn't have any clue about the Agha Netra.

A worried Bijoy with the other seven went back to Saint Anityo's house. At his house he received a call from someone who was watching him.

"Bijoy, is it you?" the voice whispered.

"Yes," Bijoy replied wondering who was it.

"The messenger of nine, searching for a promise which was lost long back. Is it you, Bijoy?" the muffled voice asked.

Bijoy was shocked to hear when he was addressed as a messenger. Again, Bijoy confirmed his identity to him.

"Who are you?" Bijoy asked with authority.

"Your reflection. Your inner soul. I came here to remind you about the power of the Unknowns, the power of the chosen ones," the voice convinced Bijoy.

"Before I say something, I want you to listen a story. One story that highlights the significance of reminding someone of their promise, commitment and power," he continued mysteriously.

"When Lord Rama's beloved wife, Sita, was abducted by the demon king Ravana, Lord Rama embarked on a dangerous journey to rescue her. Along the way, he encountered numerous challenges and sought the support of various allies, including the mighty monkey warrior, Hanuman.

"During their search for Sita, Lord Rama and his army faced a formidable obstacle – a vast ocean that stood between them and the demon kingdom of Lanka, where Sita was held captive. During this moment of despair, Lord Rama was reminded of his divine connection with the ocean god, Varuna. Seeking assistance, he performed a sacred ritual and appealed to Varuna to help bridge the vast expanse of water.

"However, when the ritual appeared to be ineffective, Lord Rama was disheartened. It was then that Hanuman, ever devoted and unwavering in his commitment to Lord Rama, stepped forward. Hanuman, with his extraordinary strength and faith, decided to leap across the ocean, believing that his devotion would carry him to his goal.

"As Hanuman prepared to make the tremendous leap, the other vanaras began to express their doubts, questioning whether he could truly accomplish such a feat. Hanuman, filled with determination, reassured them of his capabilities and invoked the name of Lord Rama, declaring that his unwavering devotion would guide him through any challenge.

"With the entire army watching, Hanuman took a colossal leap, soaring through the sky with boundless courage. As he reached the middle of the vast ocean, doubts once again began to cloud his mind. It was then that the mighty demon king, Surasa, rose from the depths of the sea, blocking Hanuman's path.

"Surasa, seeing Hanuman's extraordinary abilities, challenged him to enter her mouth and fulfil her hunger. However, Hanuman, ever mindful of his purpose, politely declined and requested that Surasa allow him to continue his journey uninterrupted.

"Surasa persisted, insisting that it was her duty to test Hanuman's resolve. Unyielding, Hanuman transformed his size to expand his body to unimaginable proportions, leaving Surasa no choice but to enlarge her mouth to accommodate him. At that very moment, Hanuman swiftly shrank back to his original size, effortlessly evading Surasa's grasp.

"Witnessing this incredible display of loyalty and cleverness, Surasa was astounded and granted Hanuman permission to continue his mission. Hanuman, true to his promise and guided by his unwavering commitment, successfully reached the demon kingdom of Lanka, ultimately playing a pivotal role in the rescue of Sita.

"This tale as a reminder of the power of determination, devotion, and reminding others of their promise. It exemplifies how unwavering commitment, even in the face of doubts and obstacles, can lead to the fulfilment of one's duties and the achievement of extraordinary feats."

Bijoy was mesmerized with the voice and the words filled him with the commitment to identify his true strength and find the Agha Netra.

"Who are you?" Bijoy asked him.

"All the nine of us believe in you. Find the Agha Netra. It is the purpose of life for all Unknowns. This is the reason why you are born."

The call ended.

Bijoy quickly scanned the recent call list but strangely there was no number in list. There was no evidence that someone had even called him.

One of the seven Unknowns tapped his shoulder.

"I got a tip that someone powerful from the triad has reached here. We have to move fast Bijoy, let's get the letter and find the Agha Netra."

"As long as they don't know that we are here to find the Agha Netra as well, this is our battle with our fate. But once they come to know about us, it will turn into a ruthless chase. Then either the Agha Netra will be found to be protected or it will be lost forever in the hands of traitors." Bijoy looked across the door staring at the Buddha statue.

***

The weather of Mussoorie was proving to be harsh on the old and weakened bodies of the seven. One of the seven had fallen sick. The others decided that he should stay at Anityo's ashram to rest. The remaining seven decided to go out in search of the Agha Netra. Few possessed the stamina that they needed to search for the Agha Netra. Bijoy was the fittest among them.

The seven were in desperate need of a clue, and based on Kevin's input, the only way was get one was from Sana's letter. It was obvious that Sana would not handover the letter to them. They would have to steal it from her. None other than Kevin was identified for the job.

Bijoy called Kevin.

"We have a job for you. Steal that letter and bring it to us."

"I can't. That letter is close to Sana heart. She trusts me, and I am in no mood to break that trust."

Kevin sounded reluctant.

"Kevin, slowly things are getting out of control and even out of my hand. We don't have time. I'm losing my patience. Let trust get broken rather than someone's neck," Bijoy hissed.

"You have time till tonight. Get me the letter by then."

"What will you give me in return?" Kevin was adamant.

"Do you think you have the option to negotiate?"

Bijoy smiled, and he hung up.

While talking to Bijoy, Kevin was standing at a distance from Sana. They both were near Slyverton ground, a historical site from the freedom struggle.

Kevin looked at Sana and told himself, "Sorry Sana, this friend is going to betray you to save your life."

Sana was randomly inquiring about her grandfather. She was unaware that those cottages were built on a significant historical ground. She sneaked into a cottage to inquire about her grandfather, and there, to her surprise, she saw a picture of her grandfather with few other people standing nearby. After an initial enquiry she got to know that people standing near her grandfather were freedom fighters who lived together. And the cottage now belonged to the grandson one of those freedom fighters. She spoke to the owner of the cottage, and it turned out his grandfather and Sana's grandfather had been good friends.

"Yes, they indeed knew each other very well. There is a diary in which my grandfather had written about his freedom struggle days."

He got up to fetch it. He returned with the old diary and handed it over to her.

The diary looked as if it was almost a hundred years old. The pages had turned yellow and were fragile. The cover, made of leather, was worn out and had faded initials on it. Sana cautiously started to flip the pages. She didn't find any evidence about her grandfather or his friends using fire arms. She found no evidence as such in the notes. Every page was talking about Gandhian thoughts and how they could be used to spread unity among the people to fight against the British.

"Unfortunately, I can't find what I am looking for," Sana said and handed back the diary to the person.

"What are you looking for?" the person asked taking back the diary.

"Nothing, I was wrong. I thought my grandfather had used weapons at some point of time. But there is no mention of it anywhere. If our grandfathers were always together, then there would have been a mention of it," Sana said dejectedly.

The person smiled and went back inside. After a while he brought a few envelopes and gave them to Sana.

"They did have weapons hidden somewhere, but they never used them."

Sana was worried. If the letters did mention the weapons hidden somewhere, it meant what her grandfather had written in that cryptic letter would start to make sense. Sana opened the envelopes and started reading the letters. They were exchanges between other revolutionaries and them. They were asked to keep the weapon handy in case they needed firearms to tear the eardrums of the Britishers so that they could hear the deafening roar for freedom.

A war cry for independence. Complete independence.

The words gave Sana goosebumps.

It was hard to believe that her Baba would have had other means to achieve their goal for freedom. It was a discovery for Sana. A big revelation that nobody knew in her family so far. Sana was happy that no one could say her Baba had lost his senses while writing the letter. He had written a letter with a hidden meaning. She returned to the hotel with Kevin.

"I am glad that he was not insane or crazy as some people called him," Sana said with a sign of relief.

"Yes, indeed. I told you he was a genius," Kevin replied convincing Sana.

"So, what next? We need to figure out what is the purpose of this letter. What message he wanted to convey."

Sana was anxious.

"See, I can give it a thought. You leave this letter with me tonight. Let me decode it further," Kevin proposed.

Sana was hesitant. It was the only memorabilia which she had from her Baba. It meant a lot to her.

Kevin understood Sana's concern. He reassured her that he'd keep the letter well guarded. Kevin promised to keep it safe and return it to her as soon as he was done decoding it. It was difficult, but Sana decided to trust Kevin and gave him the letter.

That night Sana left the Golden Gate Hotel, with the belief that next morning, when she would come to work, Kevin would return the letter with some more information to reveal the secret her Baba hid in the letter.

Chapter 19

Time for Revelation

"Do you have it?" Bijoy asked.

"Yes, I have. But I will only give it you if you promise that you will not touch any of us – Rajat, Alisha and Sana or me. You will not cross our paths again," Kevin said in an authoritative voice.

"As you wish, master," Bijoy giggled. "You try not to come near us or else you know..." Bijoy added.

But then Kevin felt a pang of guilt and betrayal deep within as he handed the letter to Bijoy. He knew he had crossed a line and had broken the trust of someone he cared about. The weight of his actions weighed heavily on his conscience, causing him to question his judgment and regret his decision. He wished he could turn back the clock and undo his mistake. He knew that repairing the damage would be a difficult journey ahead.

Bijoy was unaware that the letter would need someone who could decrypt those words. He did not know that the messenger of the letter himself would be of help. As soon as Kevin left, he read it. Bijoy's brows furrowed in confusion and frustration as he read the letter again and again. The words on the page seemed jumbled and nonsensical, leaving him utterly bewildered. He couldn't comprehend why Kevin had handed him such a perplexing piece of writing.

***

Anityo was in his ashram thinking all about the story of Kamla and her daughter Alisha. He was still not sure whether Alisha had seen the same box in her dream. He thought of meeting Alisha to know for himself.

"Believe nothing, no matter where you read it, or who says it, no matter if I have said it, unless it agrees with your own reason and your own common sense."

A soft voice disturbed the calmness of the room. The calmness around the Buddha statue in the lotus position was reflecting the serenity that was attained through meditation. The lotus was a symbol of purity and spiritual enlightenment, creating an atmosphere of tranquillity and inner peace.

Arini walked into the room as if she owned the place. Anityo was in shocked to see her in his ashram.

"Anityo, prove me wrong by showing me how useful you are. We are well aware of your worthlessness."

Arini chuckled.

"I know a girl who may know where the Agha Netra is," Anityo responded in a stammering voice.

Arini frowned "Now we are talking. Who is she?" Arini walked towards Anityo.

"Her name is Alisha."

Anityo told Arini about Alisha and her dreams. He said Alisha was a girl with an extraordinary gift, and experienced dreams so vivid and potent that they transcended into reality, blurring the lines between fantasy and the tangible world. With every dream she had, Alisha discovered her power to see what can happen next. In her last dream she had seen blood drenched hands holding the box. The Agha Netra.

"Where I can find that girl? It feels like asking her is as good as asking Google assistance on the map to find the Agha Netra!" Arini giggled. "If whatever you said is correct then, it's wonderful. However, if it turns out to be a made-up story, then I will send you directly to God in heaven to get his blessing," she threatened.

Anityo gave her Kamla's address. Without wasting any time Arini immediately sent two men to look for Alisha. When she was found,

Arini instructed them to bring her to the ashram.

Kevin had handed over the letter to Bijoy, and Anityo had given Alisha's address to Arini. The Unknowns and triad were inching towards the treasure from different directions. But before finding a path to reach the box, they had to decode a letter and a dream.

Anityo was sitting anxiously and thinking all about Arini. He dialled a number.

"See, I told her who knows about the Agha Netra. It's just a matter of days or weeks before it is found. I have got my men searching for the Agha Netra in the forests. It's a race now. A treasure hunt."

"You have to reach there first, Anityo. Your life and the Xiamen throne is at stake," the man replied before hanging up the phone.

***

Alisha and Rajat, fuelled by Alisha's dreams, embarked on a daring jungle adventure in search of the typical pattern of deodar trees. Despite Alisha's face blindness, she believed her dreams held the key to unlocking the trees' mystery which would guide her to the temple. As they delved deeper into the wilderness, Alisha's intuition guided them towards a hidden grove where the deodars stood in an intricate, mesmerizing pattern. The pattern of the trees gave her a sense of déjà vu.

Although unable to recognize Rajat's face, Alisha felt an unbreakable bond with him, trusting him completely as he described the breathtaking sight before them. As Alisha and Rajat ventured deep into the forest, the sun began to set, casting golden hues upon the lush greenery. Disappointed that they couldn't find the pattern yet, they reluctantly decided to make their way back. Alisha drew a cross on a few trees to mark the spot where they had reached.

Though their expedition didn't yield the desired results, Alisha and Rajat remained hopeful, vowing to return the next day. As they trekked through the fading light, they knew that their passion for finding the

Agha Netra would keep them driven, and they would never give up on unravelling the mystery of the deodar trees' typical pattern and to find the hidden temple.

Alisha, unaware of the looming danger, walked briskly through the dimly lit streets after her unsuccessful search for the hidden treasure of Agha Netra. Behind her, two mysterious men trailed silently, their intent unclear to her. The night grew spooky, and Alisha's heart pounded with unease, sensing she was not alone. With adrenaline coursing through her veins, she quickened her pace to reach home. She was terrified. Why were the men following her?

She called Sana after reaching home and narrated the story to her, however not revealing why she was out so late at night. Sana decided to meet Alisha in the morning to see what could be done next.

As the morning sun streamed through her window, Sana couldn't wait any longer and dialled Kevin's number, brimming with curiosity. She had to ask if he had decoded the letter.

To her dismay, Kevin's voice sounded troubled as he confessed, "I'm sorry, Sana, but I've lost the letter. I think I left it in the cafe but when I went to look for it again, it was not there."

Fear and frustration gripped Sana's heart upon learning that Kevin had lost the crucial letter. Unable to contain her emotions, she lashed out in anger and asked him to meet her at the lobby of the hotel.

Kevin realized the impact of his mistake. He understood the weight of her emotions and knew she was shattered to the core. Feeling sorry, he was determined to take responsibility for his actions and promised to tell her the truth if the situation spiralled out of control. He couldn't bear the thought of hiding the truth from her, valuing their trust and friendship above everything else. With a heavy heart, he prepared to face the consequences of his actions and hoped for a chance to make things right.

Sana reached the hotel.

"What have you done, Kevin? I trusted you completely."

As tears streamed down Sana's cheeks, she bared her soul to Kevin, revealing the letter's significance. It was the only evidence that could prove Baba wasn't crazy and had important revelations to share before he left the world. Kevin was all ears, realizing the gravity of his mistake. Still, he was determined to make amends. He promised Sana that he would do everything in his power to find the lost letter.

"Kevin, you broke my trust, and our friendship is shattered," Sana said.

"I am sorry, Sana. How could I be so careless? It's all my fault and I will do whatever it takes to find the letter," Kevin begged.

"I don't think I can meet you again, Kevin. I think that's it. It was all my fault that I trusted you. Now I have to pay for it!" Sana said and started to walk out of the lobby..

Kevin was not ready to lose Sana.

"Sana! Wait!" he shouted to stop her.

Sana paused for a few seconds then started to walk out again.

Kevin shouted again.

"I know where the letter is. I gave it away. I promise I will give it back to you."

Sana turned around, walked swiftly towards Kevin and gave him a tight slap.

"You thief! Give my letter back!" Sana yelled at him.

"It's not with me now, but I promise I will get it back. Just let me tell you I did it to save the lives of all four of us."

"What? Four?" Sana looked puzzled.

"Yes. Me, you, Alisha and Rajat. The letter contains a lot more than what you think, Sana. Your Baba has hidden a treasure box, and the location is in the letter. And someone powerful is in town who is in desperate to find that box which contains the Agha Netra. If I did not give him that letter, we all would have been in deep trouble," Kevin said solemnly.

There was a long silence.

Sana took a couple of minutes to understand what he had said.

While Kevin was speaking to Sana, someone tapped his shoulder. It was Bijoy and his men, much to his shock. Bijoy, fuming with frustration demanded an explanation for the senseless letter.

"Is this some kind of joke?" Bijoy was frustrated and angry. Meanwhile, Sana stood watching them in surprise.

"I will explain everything about the letter, Bijoy."

Kevin revealed that the letter was actually a cleverly encrypted message, leading to something which was hidden. He tried to convince Bijoy that the contents in the letter indicated where the Agha Netra was.

Bijoy appeared unconvinced by Kevin's explanation and questioned why he believed the letter was connected to the Agha Netra.

Kevin, with a knowing smile, revealed a piece of evidence. The eye that pointed directly at the Agha Netra's involvement in the mysterious web of words, leaving Bijoy astonished. Kevin also quoted the example of hidden arms which Sana's grandfather was talking about in the secret letter.

"In case what you are saying is correct, Kevin, then we have a cryptic map in our hands. But if you are wrong, then there will be hell to pay," Bijoy warned.

Sana quickly stood up and ran towards the letter which Bijoy was holding. It was the same letter which her Baba has written. Her worry started to fade away, and a smile returned to her face.

It was her Baba's letter. And Kevin was spilling the beans about the letter and its intent. That fuelled more anger in Sana when she looked at him. At the same moment he briefly looked at Sana.

"I can help you find Agha Netra, but you will have to let Sana go and return the letter to her. Keep Sana out of it!" Kevin begged.

Bijoy was in a state of indifference, unwilling to consider any request. He found himself caught between belief and skepticism as he heard Kevin's story about the mysterious letter penned by Sana's Baba. Just as this was unfolding, Bijoy received a call from Anityo's ashram, informing him that one of the Unknowns was seriously ill. Anityo asked Bijoy urgently to come down and admit him to the hospital.

"We have to go now, Kevin. And you don't have any choice but to come with us. There is a problem," Bijoy said curtly.

Kevin looked at Sana as she shook her head to say 'no'.

Bijoy looked at Sana and handed over the letter to her.

"Sana, I can sense the feeling that it might be Shiva's wish for me to tell you about us and the Agha Netra. Take this letter, it's yours. But you and Kevin will have to come with us. There is a secret that you should know about us. About the Unknowns."

The other Unknowns with Bijoy were surprised. The messenger never mentioned the Agha Netra to a person alien to that group. But it was their sheer belief in the messenger that stopped them from questioning him.

They soon reached Anityo's ashram. The Unknown who lying on the bed was gasping. He looked at Bijoy and asked him to come near him.

He said, "Bijoy, as you face my last moments, I beg of you to consider bringing new blood into the group. This group needs people who can support you."

Bijoy asked, "Is it important to discuss that at this time?"

The Unknown replied, "I am leaving, and it's crucial for the group's future. Also, promise me you'll complete your task of finding the Agha Netra. It holds the key to our legacy."

Bijoy looked at Sana and Kevin, and then back at the Unknown.

"I have hope that the younger members will grasp our legacy and will be willing to make sacrifices. We all know the history of Arinjay, the traitor, and I am afraid to take another chance. The trust I have in all seven of you is not easily found in someone new."

"I am afraid. What if I make the wrong choice?" he added.

All of a sudden, Bijoy felt the hand of the Unknown he was holding slip away. A spooky silence engulfed the room as a realization hit them; the eighth Unknown had departed, leaving them now as a group of seven.

Sana and Kevin witnessed the scene unfolding before their eyes. It was filled with dread and gloom. Someone had just left the world.

As the evening sky dimmed, Bijoy concluded the solemn last rites and sought out Sana and Kevin to reveal an ancient tale. He embarked on a narration about the Agha Netra, a powerful entity masked in mystery, and the elusive group known as the Nine Unknowns. Remarkably, this was the first instance where a messenger divulged his identity without adhering to the customary rituals, signifying the gravity of the situation.

Throughout the evening, Bijoy poured his heart and soul into explaining the intricate details of the saga that intertwined the Agha Netra, Arinjay, and the enigmatic triad. His eager hope rested on Sana and Kevin's shoulders as he extended an invitation for them to join the Nine Unknowns. However, this privileged invitation came with a grave condition: utmost secrecy. Bijoy emphasized that the knowledge of their identities, as well as the profound truths of the Agha Netra must remain confined solely to him.

Sana was determined to prove that the letter written by her Baba had a specific purpose, and she saw this as a perfect opportunity to do so. Kevin, who had already betrayed the trust of those close to him in the past, believed that supporting Bijoy would be a chance to regain that lost trust. Without fully realizing it, both Sana and Kevin found themselves with compelling reasons to join Bijoy and the group of Nine Unknowns. As the night grew darker, Sana and Kevin separately made the decision to become part of the mysterious group. Little did they know that they were entering into a legacy hidden from the world, safeguarding something incredibly powerful beyond their imagination.

The painful memory of Arinjya's betrayal haunted Bijoy, and he couldn't forget the grave mistake made by their predecessor. Faced with uncertainty, Bijoy made a momentous decision to initiate Sana and Kevin into the ranks of the Unknowns through a time-honoured ritual. The following day, he invited both of them to come down to Anityo's ashram, where the customary ceremony would take place.

As the evening descended, a crackling bonfire was set ablaze, and the six individuals formed a circle around it, but this circle was notably smaller than before. Sana and Kevin sat at a distance, their eyes fixed on the dancing flames. Bijoy beckoned them to come closer to the fire, where he began to reveal the secrets of their existence and the enigmatic mysterious Agha Netra. He spoke with solemnity, explaining that they must swear endless loyalty to the seven Unknowns and vow never to abandon the group, with the only way out being through death.

Sana, determined to uncover the purpose behind her Baba's letter, took the vow without hesitation, and Kevin followed suit. This moment was utterly surreal for Sana, as she never could have imagined that the same girl who once desired to pursue her MBA at a prestigious US university, would now stand pledging to become a part of a secret legacy. The gravity of the situation sent shivers down her spine, and her heart raced faster than she ever thought possible. Despite the intensity of the moment, Sana was fully absorbed in the process of joining this ancient and mysterious legacy.

By taking this oath, Sana and Kevin were now bound to the fate of the Nine Unknowns. The weight of responsibility now rested on their shoulders, as they became custodians of secrets and guardians of a powerful legacy concealed from the world. Little did they know the challenges, adventures, and revelations that awaited them in this fascinating journey to find the Agha Netra.

After the ritual, Sana stood there, gazing at the Sanskrit word 'Swagamah' which meant 'Welcome,' illuminated by the warm orange flames of the bonfire. In that moment, she looked truly beautiful, and Kevin couldn't help but wish to pause time and keep admiring her. He smiled, realizing that joining the Unknowns meant he could stay close to Sana, whom he had fallen for countless times before. Lost in her thoughts, Sana was brought back to reality when Kevin spoke.

He expressed his unwavering loyalty to her, though acknowledging that she might not give him a chance to prove it. Kevin would always be there for her, regardless of her feelings towards him.

Sana responded with a smirk, hinting her own reasons for being there. Her main reason was to prove that her Baba was not mentally sick when he wrote the letter. Additionally, she sensed that Bijoy needed their assistance too. Beyond that, she wished for a life away from people who pretended to be trustworthy and true friends but were, in reality, fake and insincere.

Chapter 20

Quest for the Agha Netra

"Shall we start begin the search again?" Rajat gazed at Alisha.

Alisha silently nodded in agreement, but her expression revealed her concerns.

"What's troubling you? It seems like something is weighing on your mind," Rajat said, taking a deep breath before continuing, "Is it about me? Do you still believe you cannot trust me?"

"A few days ago, after we returned from the jungle, I noticed two men following me. Now, I'm worried. It appears that we might have stumbled upon something far more dangerous than we think. If those men are tailing me, it suggests we are not alone in this search," Alisha revealed her fears.

"I don't mean to dismiss your suspicion, but it might be possible that it is just a delusion. They could be random strangers walking down the street," Rajat tried to persuade Alisha.

"I'm certain they're not, Rajat. I can feel it in my gut that I'm being followed. But who are they?" Alisha remained anxious.

"After today's search, I'll make sure to take you back home. If they were following you before, chances are they'll do the same today," Rajat assured her, offering his firm support.

Once again, they embarked on their hike towards the heart of the jungle. The winding paths amidst the deodar trees felt like a perplexing maze, where one wrong turn could lead you back to where you started. For Rajat, being in Alisha's company was always a delight. Their conversations flowed naturally, and he made sure to express himself honestly while being considerate not to hurt Alisha in any way. To help her recognize him effortlessly, he decided to wear the same blue t-shirt and light blue jeans daily. Every day. Everything remained unchanged since the beginning of their quest to find the box. He didn't want Alisha to feel burdened by her face blindness, and so he did his best to provide her with comfort and reassurance throughout their journey.

"Hey, look over here! Can you see these marks? I actually made them when we were here last time!" Alisha exclaimed with joy as she and Rajat reached the exact same spot they had turned back from during their previous visit. Alisha couldn't contain her excitement and stood there for a few minutes, taking in the familiar surroundings. She closed her eyes for a moment, allowing the memories of her dream to flood her mind.

As she reminisced, Alisha reached into her pocket and retrieved a piece of paper. On it was a drawing she had made earlier, along with some writing. It was fascinating to see that the place matched her dream so perfectly. Next, they had to locate the small temple that she believed existed nearby.

Rajat, concerned for Alisha, approached her and stood by her side. "Are you okay?" he asked worriedly.

With a smile, Alisha reassured him, "Yes, I'm fine. This is the exact place I dreamt about. Now, the next step is to find that temple. It is puzzling how nobody seems to know about the existence of the temple in this modern world. It is like a hidden place, unexplored and unknown. How is that even possible?"

Rajat carefully observed their surroundings, trying to decipher the identity of the person who had hidden the box in that location. It was evident that this individual had taken great pains to ensure that the box remained well-concealed, making its discovery a challenging task. The tall deodar trees loomed overhead, casting peculiar shadows that seemed to play tricks on the eye. The dense forest felt like a maze, where even the most seasoned explorers could easily lose their way.

Feeling a sense of urgency, Alisha emphasized the need to act swiftly and exit the jungle before sunset. Time was of the essence, and they couldn't afford to linger any longer in this mysterious and potentially dangerous place.

After walking for an hour Rajat and Alisha stumbled upon quite a sight: a small plateau nestled amidst the surrounding terrain. It stuck out like an island suddenly emerging in the sea. The unexpected discovery left them both surprised. They couldn't help but voice their amazement simultaneously, "What is that?"

Driven by curiosity Rajat approached the towering wall of the plateau, which loomed twenty metres high. As he gently touched the wall, some fine particles became dislodged and fell to the ground. Turning to Alisha he asked, "Have you ever come across something like this in your dreams?"

After taking a brief pause to reflect, Alisha responded, "As far as I can remember, I've never seen this plateau in my dreams. It's possible that it might have made a fleeting appearance in one of those dreams where I find myself running through a forest of log trees, but it wasn't noteworthy enough to be firmly imprinted in my memory."

Talking about it, they both reached the plateau and touched it with bare hands. It was made of solid sediments and looked like it had been there since ages. They looked around but there was no sign of any temple. The eyes which looked deep into the deodar trees did not find any sign of a temple or temple spire. It was a quiet and deep jungle. They realized that if they lost their way, it would be difficult to go back.

"Let's rest here for a while and then we will go back. Looks like we have to begin from the start tomorrow," Alisha said and went near the wall of the plateau.

"It won't be an easy task as I thought it would be. I am wondering is it possible that while you are dreaming, you can suddenly go to a different location and not even realize it?" Rajat looked at Alisha.

"What I want to say is that imagine you were running in this jungle among the tall deodar trees but then suddenly you find yourself in another place and there you see a temple and then those hands."

"If these dreams are showing me the real world, then that will not happen. Unless what I dream is not is going to happen in the future." Alisha took a deep breath.

"That box is making the dream a reality," she added.

They rest their backs on the wall of plateau and Alisha took out a bottle of water. Rajat looked at her.

"Can I have some?"

"Sorry Rajat. I do not share my water bottle," Alisha said and pulled out a disposable water bottle from her bag and extended it towards Rajat.

Rajat smiled.

"Thanks. At least you have another one."

They smiled at each other and Rajat kept the water bottle next to him. After a while they stood up and started to walk back home.

"I hope today those men don't follow me."

Alisha looked worried.

"Even if they come in front of me, I won't remember their faces next time. You have to identify yourself Rajat, just in case I don't recognize you. And I might mistake you for those mysterious men," she added.

Rajat smiled.

Suddenly Rajat said, "Hey wait, I forgot my water bottle at the plateau."

And he ran back towards the plateau to get his bottle back.

Alisha waited for him to come back.

Ten minutes had passed, and there was still no sign of Rajat. Alisha couldn't help feeling increasingly worried and anxious. The place where Rajat had left the bottle wasn't too far away from where she stood, and this proximity only heightened her concern. Alisha started to retrace her steps to see if she could find him.

As Alisha walked for a few minutes, her heart raced with every step she took. Eventually, she reached the plateau and, to her surprise, saw Rajat standing there, as if frozen in time, with his back turned towards her. In an attempt to get his attention, she decided to call out his name, hoping that he would respond or turn around to acknowledge her, but Rajat remained unmoved and unresponsive.

***

At Anityo's ashram, Sana who was newly inducted into the Nine Unknowns was meeting with the other members. The age of each member was nearing seventy years. Sana who was in search of proving her Baba's worth was among a group that needed care and support. She soon started to feel at home among them.

Bijoy was sitting with Kevin and they both were trying to figure out what the letter had to say about the location.

"I know he mentioned the pattern of trees and hidden weapons. But it's hard to go on from there. These words are difficult to decode.

It's all black, she is black, he is black and black is your soul. She resides in a place which is hard to explore. The dwelling has a spear, and she killed him and his peers. Her husband drank Halāhala and saved the world by lying down at her feet.

One of the Unknowns spoke up.

"Halāhala is the poison which Shiva drank after it was discovered during Samudra Manthan. But why he is lying down at someone's feet to save the world?"

"Once, there was a powerful and fearsome demon named Raktabija, who terrorized the world with his evil deeds. Every drop of his blood that fell on the ground would give rise to a new demon, making it impossible to defeat him. The gods sought help from the divine Mother Kali, the embodiment of fierce energy," he continued.

"Ma Kali, with her dark complexion, wild hair, and fierce demeanour, took on the challenge. She entered the battlefield, armed with her sword and trident, and waged a fierce battle against Raktabija. However, with each drop of his blood that fell, the demon's strength multiplied.

Seeing the situation become dire, Lord Shiva intervened. He lay down in the path of Kali's destructive rampage, hoping to stop her. As Kali danced her wild dance of destruction, her foot accidentally touched Shiva's chest. Realizing her mistake and the potential consequences, she stuck out her tongue in shame and sorrow.

"This act of sticking out her tongue stunned Kali, and she calmed down. Shiva's intervention broke the cycle of Raktabija's bloodshed. With Kali's wrath and Shiva's compassion working together, they finally defeated the demon.

"From that moment on, Ma Kali and Lord Shiva became a revered duo, representing the perfect balance of destructive and nurturing forces. Kali is worshiped as the fierce and protective mother, while Shiva is honoured as the serene and benevolent father. Their combined energy reminds us that destruction is necessary for new creations, and compassion tempers the fierceness of power. Together, they embody the eternal cycle of life and death, creation, and destruction.

"Every drop created a new demon. That's what peers means. That is so cryptic," Kevin said quietly. She dwells in a place with spears?" he asked.

"I have no idea about it," the Unknown said and lay down on the bed.

"Every temple has a spear. Does it mean a Kali temple?" he asked.

"Yes, must be a Kali temple. In the past, people used to hide their weapons in a Kali temple. I am sure her baba had hidden the weapons in the temple. We are sure to find a clue there." Kevin was prompt.

"So, it's the pattern of deodar trees and Kali temple where the weapons are hidden," Bijoy said thoughtfully.

"But why we are searching for weapons?" One of the Unknowns asked.

"There might be some clue, about the Agha Netra. If Baba had the Agha Netra, he might have decided to hide it with weapons," Bijoy replied.

"Let us not waste any time and commence this journey. If you think that the triad is nearby, then we must act quickly," stated Kevin.

Bijoy looked at the five Unknowns; two of them were weak. Among them, only three were in a reasonable state of health, which was essential for an endeavour demanding stamina and physical prowess. Although they had a considerable amount of determination, it wasn't sufficient to overcome their physical limitations.

Looking at Kevin, Bijoy responded, "When you were here, I had a group of men who were monitoring your movements. But as you are among us, and we are progressing towards the correct path to locate the Agha Netra, I no longer have faith in their loyalty. I have relieved them of their responsibilities to follow you. It's just us now – the true guardians of the Agha Netra. This expedition is now solely our responsibility. We must continue the journey alone from this point onward."

Curious, Sana inquired, "What is it that you would like us to do next?"

"I have singled out three individuals from our group of five who will come with us in the pursuit. The remaining two will stay behind and rest," explained Bijoy.

Bijoy engaged in a conversation with Anityo, inquiring about a location he might be familiar with – one concealed within a dense and uncharted jungle. Alternatively, he questioned whether he had any knowledge of a Kali temple nestled amid the profound jungle of deodar trees. Unfortunately, Anityo lacked knowledge of such specific places, though he could at least identify regions characterized by thick, untouched deodar trees. This endeavour felt akin to a blind attempt, hoping the thrown dart would miraculously strike the target. With no other alternatives available, they found themselves compelled to embrace this uncertainty and take the risk.

"Bijoy, where are you off to?" inquired Anityo.

"I'm on a search to uncover something that has been awaiting us for a long time. The end of this anticipation is getting closer," Bijoy responded with unwavering assurance.

"May the blessings of Lord Shiva accompany you on this expedition," Anityo grinned.

Bijoy's enigmatic reply piqued Anityo's curiosity. Though he refrained from sounding too snoopy, he couldn't resist asking,

"But what is it precisely?"

"It's something that needs to be discovered to be protected and safeguarded," Bijoy said smiling, as he departed the ashram accompanied by six companions, leaving two behind.

Anityo's initial reaction, filled with surprise, was a single word echoing in his mind: 'Agha Netra!' It was difficult for him to come to terms with the fact that he had provided shelter to the Nine Unknowns. Despite his long acquaintance with Bijoy, never had he suspected that he might be one of the Unknowns. The truth remained unclear: was Bijoy indeed among the unknown individuals? If so, Anityo found himself trapped in a difficult dilemma; caught between a rock and a hard place. One side there was a long known friend and on the other, Arini, the hungry lioness whose thirst to concur the throne of the triad bought her in search of the Agha Netra.

Kevin steered the car towards the location Anityo had directed. After covering a few kilometres, an unexpected sight greeted them: a makeshift police checkpoint. Perplexed, he pulled over, and the police instructed them to park the vehicle on the side. Bijoy's voice carried weight as he inquired, "What's happening here?"

"We're on the lookout for a shooter," replied the police. Deep down, Bijoy worried that the triad might have struck again, possibly taking another life in their relentless search for the Agha Netra.

"Who was shot? Do you have a description of the shooter? Any reason behind it?" Bijoy asked with evident concern.

"He's a young boy named Arvind. He shot a well-known businessman in town," the police explained while inspecting their car.

Sana's familiarity with the name prompted her to interject, "Arvind, is he a canteen boy?"

The police momentarily halted their search, fixing their gaze on Sana. One of them inquired, "Yes, do you know him?"

"Yes, he works at MJK. But why did he shoot a businessman? Arvind is a simple boy. It is impossible for me to believe that he has shot someone!" Sana was baffled.

The policeman replied, "The reason we will only come to know when he is caught."

Every experience you're currently going through is actually getting you ready for what you've been seeking, Bijoy said to himself after he heard the conversation between Sana and the policeman.

"It will take you about an hour to get there. Then we will start exploring the deodar woods and, if we are lucky, we might find the temple," Kevin told Sana.

Having driven for an hour, they arrived at the designated spot described by Anityo. They found themselves at the edge of a dense jungle. However, due to the limited visibility in the dim light, the task of locating the deodar trees and identifying any tree patterns appeared to be an insurmountable challenge.

They started to walk into the jungle, closely looking around the trees to find the specific pattern which was described in the letter. They were grouped in the shape of a triangle. One at each corner. Every eye was looking at the trees and footsteps were firmly kept on the ground. They kept their ears open in case someone found the trees first and called out to the rest.

"It's mysterious. We can keep walking deep into the jungle, but as more trees come our way, finding that pattern will be harder."

After walking for an hour, they arrived at a place where they noticed a few cross marks on the trees. It was evident that someone had intentionally marked the deodar trees in a specific manner. Bijoy approached the marks and wondered aloud, "Do these trees match the pattern mentioned in the letter?"

Kevin examined the marks closely and responded, "Yes, it seems to resemble the same pattern. If you observe the first tree, there's a triangular arrangement. It's definitely the same pattern!" Kevin expressed his joy and excitement.

Suddenly, one of the three Unknowns posed an unexpected question that left everyone surprised. "Who do you think made these marks? Bijoy, could it be the work of the triad?"

These questions introduced a worrying possibility. If these marks were indeed on the trees Bijoy was seeking, then the concern arose about who had arrived there first. Doubts crept in, suggesting that if the triad had reached the location ahead of them, they might have also reached the temple. The worst-case scenario would involve them discovering the Agha Netra's location.

Sana attempted to bolster their spirits, saying, "Let's not lose hope. The temple should be around here. We can't assume they'll get there before us."

She directed her words towards Bijoy.

With new determination, they ventured further into the jungle, clinging to the hope of stumbling upon the temple soon.

As the day was turning into evening and darkness was setting in, there was still no sign of the temple. Numerous questions filled their minds. Were they following the correct path? Could the markings have been a trick to mislead them, making them lose their way? Perhaps the temple had existed once but was no longer there?

They chose to halt and to take a decision. Should they stay in the jungle, a situation they weren't prepared for? Or should they try again the next day? Everyone agreed with the latter suggestion, and they turned back, intending to return the next day.

***

On the other side of the jungle, Alisha became concerned when she noticed that Rajat was unresponsive. Approaching him, she gently shook his hand.

"I've been calling you, can't you hear me?" she asked.

Rajat stared at Aisha with a serious expression. He pointed towards a hole in the plateau that was big enough for a person to crawl through. There seemed to be a strange emptiness inside, and sunlight shone into the hole, creating bright yellow beams. If you looked closely, you could see a figure that seemed to be part monkey on the bottom and part human on the top. It was as if someone was quickly turning a light on and off, shining it on the figure's face.

Aisha also stood there, peering inside the hole. She asked, "What's that place? It seems like someone is living there. Who's shining the light on that person's face? What's happening?"

Rajat answered, "There's something hidden in the plateau, and someone has put a light inside."

After they both looked inside, they said together, "Could this be the temple we're looking for?"

"Did you see this in your dream?"

"It's tough to remember dreams clearly. They are like pictures or movies when you first see them, but later they turn into faded memories," Alisha replied.

"But I definitely remember seeing a temple. It could be the one we're looking at now," she said and continued to gaze at the light inside.

However, now she understood why Rajat was frozen when he saw this sight.

They faced a dilemma – whether they should go inside the hole to see what was inside or look for another way to go in. They decided to find an alternate route to discover what was inside of the hollow room.

They looked around carefully but found nothing and returned to the same place where they had started.

Although it was hard to take their eyes off the cave, Alisha told Rajat that there was no point standing there. They decided to mark the place and return the next day. This time they would be prepared to stay longer and discover what was inside the cave.

Chapter 21

The First Move

Anityo was taken aback when he realized that he was now hosting the Nine Unknowns. On one hand, there was a fierce triad and a hungry lioness ready to pounce on anyone in her path in search of the Agha Netra, and on the other, he had his old friend under his protection, and it was his duty to shield him from the triad – the same Xiamen goons who had cruelly taken the life of innocent Joy.

As he entered the room where the two Unknowns were sleeping, Anityo realized that Bijoy had left them behind due to their weakened state. They weren't in a condition to join the journey, like the weaker lions in a pride.

While he looked at them, contemplating how to find a solution in this situation, a voice startled him from behind, speaking in a hushed tone. It was Arini, standing right behind Anityo.

Upon hearing that voice and seeing Arini so close, Anityo couldn't help but feel a shiver down his spine – it was the last thing he expected.

Arini's question followed, "Who are they?"

Anityo's response stuttered out, "They're my guests. They are tourists."

Arini's calm and quiet tone continued, "You don't seem well, Anityo. Did I ask you something that caught you off guard? Or perhaps, like us, you're concerned about Agha Netra. After all, finding it is your responsibility too, but you haven't succeeded in your task."

Anityo was taken aback, caught between the unexpected encounter with Arini and the mounting pressure of why he was sent to Mussoorie.

"Aren't they a bit old to come to Mussoorie in this cold weather? I mean look at them." Arini frowned looking at the two sleeping men.

Anityo glanced at the Unknowns and then at Arini.

"You never know, it all about will power."

Arini smiled.

"Looks like Alisha, that girl who saw the Agha Netra in her dreams, has already started her expedition."

"I don't want her to travel alone. It's better to search for it together. The more the merrier." Arini smiled sarcastically.

"What you want to do with her?" Anityo was worried.

"Nothing, my men will bring her to my place tomorrow. So that from day after, we can all together go for the expedition. That'll be fun, won't it?" She was as sarcastic as she could be.

Arini left Anityo in a situation which was awaiting to worsen. Alisha was about to get abducted by Arini because of Anityo. Joy was killed when Anityo told the triad about him, and now Alisha's life was at stake. He was sure that once Arini found the Agha Netra, she'd kill Alisha too.

That day, late in the evening Bijoy and the others returned from the hunt empty-handed. Anityo was eager to know if Bijoy and the rest were really the Unknowns. But he on the other hand knew that even if they were really the Unknowns, Bijoy would not reveal it. So, it could only be circumstantial that they had come in search of the Agha Netra.

After dinner that night, Anityo came to Bijoy and asked him to come out for a walk.

"Why are you here, Bijoy? What are you doing in Mussoorie?" Anityo asked.

"We are here for a purpose, Anityo. It's something important for us. I am hopeful we will finish the work soon," Bijoy said confidently.

"You have lost one of your friends, still you want to stay here. What is so important in your life?" Anityo persisted.

"I know what you are wondering, Anityo," Bijoy paused and said. "Facing the departure of those one believed would stay forever is tough. Yet, one has to move on. One must. We say goodbye to our dear ones, but we must march on, not just for them but for the ones standing by our side. I am here for the rest. I am here to complete the job that we all promised ourselves to finish."

Anityo knew how tough Bijoy was. He knew that Bijoy would not easily give up neither would he reveal the reason of him being there.

"It's a tough time, Bijoy. But you are strong. You have to be strong. I don't know what you are searching for or what is your reason for being in Mussoorie is. But I can foresee times will be more challenging in the coming days. I want to tell you something that you already know." He took a deep breath.

"Challenging moments do not trouble an individual when they are struggling. It's only when those around them become aware of their struggle, that the difficulty starts to weigh on them."

What Anityo said sounded cryptic to Bijoy. He wondered why Anityo was curious to know the reason he was in Mussoorie. And also, he did mention difficult times ahead.

Either Anityo is in trouble because of me, or he wants to know the truth for a reason, he thought.

After an hour they returned to the ashram.

"Bijoy, I want to tell you something which might be useful for you," Anityo said while walking back.

"Yes, tell me," Bijoy replied looking at Anityo.

"Few weeks ago, there was a librarian named Joy. He died mysteriously. Someone said it was heart failure, and some suspected that he died because of some old illness. But there are some serious credible sources of mine who think that Joy died of poison made from a Chinese herb."

"That is quite interesting. What was the cause of death? Finally, was it discovered?" Bijoy asked.

"My source is never wrong, Bijoy. The Chinese are here."

Anityo took a deep breath and continued, "I pray you and your friends will be safe in your expedition," Anityo said and walked into the ashram.

Bijoy remained standing, a flood of thoughts running through his head.

Did Anityo know the truth? Did Anityo know that they were the Unknowns? The group which was never to be discovered... never to be found.

***

On the other side of the city, keeping his promise, Rajat decided to accompany Alsiha home. As Alisha and Rajat strolled towards her house that night, they couldn't shake the feeling of being watched. Glancing over their shoulders, they noticed a group of mysterious men trailing them. The spooky presence of the strangers added an air of mystery and unease to their journey home.

Alisha and Rajat looked at each other.

"Don't worry, I am with you. They won't do anything as long as I am here," Rajat reassured Alisha.

And after walking for a few more minutes they both reached Alisha's home. Rajat stood outside the gate and Alisha went in.

"Thank you for accompanying me till here – till I feel safe," Alisha told Rajat, smiling.

"You are always safe with me, Alisha," Rajat replied.

"Thanks for that, Rajat," Alisha started to walk into the house.

Rajat watching her go, said in slightly high voice.

"Alisha!"

Alisha stopped and looked at Rajat.

"My promises to you are very simple. I will be your one and only one best friend. I will never give up on you and promise to always be by your side. And I promise that no matter what happens or how hard times become, it will be always you and me till the very end," Rajat said in a calm voice.

Alisha's eyes locked into his and a world of unspoken feelings exchanged in those fleeting moments. With the gate half closed, she stepped outside and into his embrace, her touch conveying a depth of emotion that words could not capture. In that hug, they found solace and a connection that surpassed friendship.

***

That night Alisha remembered the conversation she had with Rajat. It felt to her that a new chapter was being unfolded within her. It was the conversations only and not the face. The pain of not remembering Rajat's face was something Alisha had to live with. That, however, did not spoil the feeling of being in a new bright world. With the warm fuzzy feeling after the magical day, she crawled into her comfy bed and drifted into a deep sleep.

That night, Alisha saw a dream that took her to a different place. In the dream, she sat on a chair, facing two elderly men who seemed fragile yet had a sense of enduring strength on their faces. Behind her stood a young woman, perhaps in her late thirties. The lady engaged in a conversation with the old men, their faces reflecting seriousness. After a while, the young woman nodded at someone nearby. Suddenly, like a bolt of lightning, that person pulled out a pistol and shot the two elderly men. The air filled with a sense of shock and fear as blood splattered in the air. It was a startling and intense moment that woke Alisha wide-eyed, with her heart racing. As she woke up, the images and emotions from the dream lingered. She could remember everything except the faces. It was three in the morning. It had happened again.

The next morning, Alisha was worried. Her mother could guess that she had seen a dream again. As Alisha and Rajat had decided to start their day early, Alisha walked out of the house after breakfast. She opened the gate and remembered the previous evening and for a moment she forgot the dreadful dream. Lost in her thoughts, she passed by a man.

"Alisha!" the man shouted.

Alisha turned and looked, trying hard to guess who he was.

"I am Rajat," Rajat said with the smile.

Alisha was not convinced. Rajat always wore the same blue t-shirt and light blue jeans. But the guy was wearing a red t-shirt and black jeans.

"Let me help you. I spilled water on that blue t-shirt and jeans. So I had to wear this."

Alisha smiled.

"Thanks for helping me out there. It's just that I cannot remember—"

Rajat stopped her.

"It doesn't matter now. As long as I am with you, I will help you to remember faces."

Alisha felt sorry for herself. Even if she wanted to remember her time with someone special, his face would always escape her memory. Falling in love with someone, yet not recognizing them in a crowd – it was quite a unique dilemma.

On the other side of the city, Anityo's calm ashram embraced serenity. The garden bloomed with diverse flowers. The peaceful ambience, gentle breeze, and natural scents offered priceless tranquillity, soothing minds and souls.

That morning Sana was standing in the garden and Kevin walked up to her.

"Hi Sana, I want to say something. I know after what I have done to you, I am the most unwanted man, but what I feel is that this search is going to be nasty and dangerous. It's just that I do not want to put you in any danger. You can opt out of this expedition. I will ensure that this letter is safe with me."

Sana looked at Kevin.

"Now this search is not only for Baba. Bijoy and the others need us in this mission."

She paused.

"And, thank you for those caring words, but it is very hard to believe you, Kevin. You might be speaking from your heart, but let time test your words," Sana added and walked inside the ashram.

After a while they all left Anityo's ashram and decided to start the journey from the point they left the search the previous day. Again the two weak Unknowns were left in Anityo's care.

***

As their journey started quite early, it didn't take them much time to reach the spot. It took them around half a day to reach a plateau which suddenly appeared from nowhere. They stopped, hearing a faint mysterious sound. It was as if a big rock had fallen somewhere in the far distance.

"I think we have lost our way. There is no sign of a temple around," Kevin said and sat on the ground.

"It will be around here. Let us take a look at the letter again," Sana suggested.

Kevin looked at the letter. Some decoding had to be done.

"There is nothing more in this letter that explains this terrain."

On the other side of the plateau, Alisha and Rajat were just putting their things down. They had found an alternate entrance to the cave, but they were running out of luck. Then suddenly something miraculous happened. A portion of the wall fell inside the cave, making a loud sound. When the dust cleared, there was a big hole, creating an easy passage.

Alisha looked at Rajat.

"I am not able to decide – did the wall collapse because it was weak or did some mysterious force cause it to crumble?"

They could hear a faint humming sound coming from inside. Rajat and Alisha stood by the cave's entrance, as they were captivated by the enigmatic melody that flowed through the walls.

"Shall we?" Rajat indicated.

Alisha nodded in agreement. They entered the mysterious cave cautiously, stepping into an unfamiliar territory filled with uncertainty and mystery.

Upon entering the cave, they found themselves in a spacious area with a flat surface. Sunlight streamed in through various holes, creating an intriguing sight. Initially, the holes seemed randomly placed, but upon closer inspection, it became evident that they were meticulously positioned. The sun's rays entered through these holes, illuminating the mirrors strategically placed, resulting in a radiant and enchanting atmosphere.

As they continued walking deeper into the cave, they were startled by a peculiar statue that blended human and animal features. The statue's head resembled that of a human, but its eyes were oddly oversized, giving it an eerie appearance. Strangely, two sabre teeth jutted out from its mouth, reminiscent of an animal's fangs. Its lips were stretched into a grin, adding to the unsettling vibe. The lower half of the statue consisted of a large stomach and disproportionately small legs that ended in claws.

This peculiar figure possessed four hands: a pair held a flower and a book, while the other set gripped a large knife and a sword. The statue was coated in red paint, though patches of it seemed to have randomly worn off in different places across its body. This combination of human and animal attributes, along with the bizarre details and the peeling red paint, created a sense of both fascination and unease.

Just behind the statue there was an idol of Kali Ma – a huge Kali Ma idol holding the creature in front of her which depicted that she had reined the creature who could create unimaginable disaster to humans.

Alisha quickly looked around to see if the Agha Netra was in the chamber. She was anxious that she should get it before Rajat did. They would be her hands instead of Rajat holding the box. But her search went in vain. There was nothing, apart from the creature and Kali Ma.

As the sun was setting and the lights on the mirror started to become dim. They had only a few hours left to find the Agha Netra which was hidden somewhere there.

Rajat who was looking at Alisha voraciously searching the place, sat near the creature. He saw a big rectangle marked on the floor. It seems to have been made by an object kept for long at one place, and then removed. It had left the impression.

"Alisha, look here!" Rajat shouted.

Alisha smiled and ran towards Rajat in excitement hoping he had found it.

"Where is it? Show me?" Alisha shouted.

Rajat showed her the mark on the floor.

"What is that?"

"It looks like there was a box or something here, and then it was removed. That has left this deep impression," Rajat said frowning.

While they were looking at the mark, a voice behind them tore the silence like a knife.

"Who are you? What are you doing here?"

Alisha and Rajat jumped in shock and turned around to see a saintly figure. His long silver hair cascaded down to his waist. He wore a flowing robe, vibrant like the sun. Wrinkles adorned his face, markers of years' wisdom. Most striking was his age; he appeared older than anyone they had encountered, perhaps surpassing a century. With closed eyes, the saint seemed immersed in meditation, stemming a calm impression, as if bound to a higher existence. Captivated, Alisha and Rajat stood enveloped in the saint's presence, feeling a peaceful connection to something beyond themselves.

"In this place, there's nothing left. Long ago, it was looted. Leave before Kaal is freed from Ma Kali and discovers you," he uttered in a ghostly tone.

Drawing close to the saint, Alisha begged, "Please, help us. We have invested all our efforts in the search for the box. My dreadful dreams are killing me day by day. This time I need to save a life."

"Alisha, if God grants your wish to remember faces, do you realize what might unfold?"

The saint's gaze held Alisha's as he continued, "You'll become a god, akin to a deity. You will save everyone in your dreams. Being God is not easy; you have to drink poison to preserve nectar."

Rajat and Alisha exchanged astonished glances when they heard the sage take Alisha's name.

"God designates each of us on earth with a purpose. We all have a reason for being here. I've lived for over a century because my purpose remains unfulfilled," the saint went on.

Alisha and Rajat hung on to every word, captivated by the saint's wisdom. His words echoed in their minds, awakening a sense of purpose and wonder within them.

"What you are searching for here is not there anymore. That container, which was filled with weapons and a mysterious box was stolen. I was here to protect the chest. I was appointed by Kaal but I failed to stop them, and Kaal closed my eyes forever," he replied.

They realized that he had lost his vision.

Rajat said, "We need to find that box. Someone's life is at stake."

"It was stolen long ago. So, I don't know where it is and I can't find it. I am cursed that I can't leave this cave."

There was dead silence in the cave and darkness gripped the interiors as the sun was about to set. The saint walked near the deity and lit the torch. He was walking around the area as if he could see everything.

Alisha and Rajat lost all hope. Their shoulders drooped in disappointment. They started to walk out from the cave. It was a dead end.

"Do not lose hope, you never know what tomorrow may bring with the new dawn," the saint called out. "Dacoits were from a tribe named Kingla. They looted the place. They were Kingla tribes that robbed everyone, even the Englishmen. They looted more Englishmen than Indians at that time. If you are able to locate them, you will find your treasure."

Both stopped in their tracks as they heard the saint's words. A ray of hope had appeared from the other end of the tunnel.

Alisha came running to the saint and bowed to him with gratitude.

"Alisha, your dreams have a purpose; once that is completed, they will be gone forever."

"And my face blindness?" Alisha was prompt in asking.

"Sometime, what you think is a curse is actually a blessing. You will realize that one day. As I said, everything in life is for a purpose."

Alisha and Rajat left the place without the Agha Netra but a clue. A tribe named Kingla.

***

The next task at hand was to find Kingla. The notorious tribe. The tribe that robbed everything, perhaps the Agha Netra as well. That night strolling through the lanes to reach home, Alisha was carefree as Rajat was with her.

"Did you ever have a girlfriend, Rajat?" Alisha smiled looking at him.

"I never tried to have one. It's hard to impress a girl," Rajat replied.

"Did you like someone earlier?" Alisha asked.

"To be fair no, I was so busy in fulfilling my dream of getting admission in to the National Law School of India that I never found time for myself." Rajat smiled.

"Do you like someone now?"

"Yes" Rajat replied

"Who is she?"

"I haven't seen her face yet."

Alisha remained quiet.

Rajat quickly realised what Alisha could infer from his words.

"Don't take it otherwise, Alisha. It's like I can feel her and I have the belief that one day I will see her and meet her."

Alisha replied, "At least, when you will meet her, you will remember her face forever."

Rajat stood there for a while and looked at Alisha. After a few steps, she stopped and looked at Rajat.

"What happened?"

Rajat smiled and replied, "You might have heard this before, but I know for sure that it's true. Love is blind. Once you fall in love, everything around you feels like and looks like the person you are in love with. You fall for a mushy heart; you fall for a lovely soul."

"That impressive, Rajat," Alisha giggled.

"And I rest my case, my lord," Rajat chuckled.

In a few minutes they reached Alisha's house. She stood near the gate and looked at Rajat.

"Thank you again."

"You don't thank a friend." Rajat smiled and walked back to his place. The euphoria and warmth filled his heart, igniting a blend of excitement and tenderness within.

Alisha reached door of her house and suddenly everything blacked out in front of her. It was as if she lost all her senses and had fallen into deep sleep suddenly.

***

On the other side of the city, Bijoy and the others returned empty-handed again. The temple was never found. They now started doubting whether they were on the right track. Were those marks on the tree made to deceive them? Or did the letter indeed not have any meaning to it?

Sana knew that Bijoy was worried about the path they were taking.

Bijoy came up to Sana.

"I still believe the letter had meaning to it. It's just that we are not able to decipher what the letter wants to say. You grandfather was truly a genius."

Sana smiled and nodded her head.

They reached Anityo's ashram late at night. Anityo was still awake and was bouncing off the wall, waiting for Bijoy.

"What happened Anityo? Is everything okay?"

"I told you Bijoy, I warned you the Chinese are here. Your two friends are missing since the evening!"

"What? Where are they? They might have gone for a walk, don't worry." Bijoy tried to calm Anityo.

"My men here saw few people walk into the ashram and carry off your friends on their shoulders!" Anityo cried wringing his hands. "They have been kidnapped!"

Bijoy was shocked; he was losing his men back-to-back.

"What? Why? I need to go to police." Bijoy was anxious.

"I don't think you will get any help there. But try your luck," Anityo replied.

***

That night at a remote place somewhere in Mussoorie, Alisha slowly opened her eyes. She saw a slim girl standing in front of her. Alisha was sitting on a chair, her hands tied behind her back. In front of her, two old men were on their knees, with their hands tied behind their backs as well.

"Hello Alisha, how are you? I am Arini from Xiamen," Arini smiled and said in a low and polite tone.

Alisha was still recovering from being unconscious. She felt weak and her body ached.

"Where am I?" Alisha stammered.

"You are with a group of people who are interested in your dreams," Arini chuckled.

That suddenly made Alisha realize that she had seen this scene before. In her dream! Two old men tied in front of her. And what terrified her was what was going to happen next.

"Arini, whatever you to ask me. I will tell you everything. But please do not kill them," Alisha begged with looking down at the floor.

"How you know I'll kill them? Did you also see that unfolding in your dream?" Arini laughed and said, "So what Anityo said was right. You can see people who are going to die." After a brief pause she continued, "Look at them, they are weak lions in Bijoy's pride. They are useless. Let them be relieved from this place."

Arini looked at the man standing near them.

Alisha looked at Arini and screamed, "No, please no! I beg you. If you kill them, I promise to myself I will choose to die rather than let you know where the Agha Netra is!"

Arini looked at the man and said, "Wait! This conversation is getting interesting. Looks like I am at the negotiation table now!" she giggled.

"What is the offer, Alisha? You hand over the Agha Netra and I will hand over these old men. Is it that simple?"

"I do not have the Agha Netra with me," Alisha replied.

"Kill them!" Arini instructed,

There was a gunshot heard and Alisha went into shock, and trembling she turned her head towards the old men.

"They are alive," Arini chuckled and continued, "Look Alisha, I have made a promise to the triad in Xiamen that they will get a new leader to lead the pack. Don't let them down. Tell me where the Agha Netra is."

"Please let them go now! And I will show you where the Agha Netra is," Alisha said in an angry voice and with authority.

"You know how risky it is to let these men go. Bijoy will be alert now that I have put my hand inside his den. But I will leave them. And you will get your freedom back when you hand over the Agha Netra to us."

Saying that Arini let the men leave.

Alisha was now a hostage in Arini's house.

Chapter 22

A Cat with Nine Lives

Bijoy's men who had been held hostage by Arini reached Anityo's ashram. At the same moment, Bijoy was leaving for the police station to lodge a complaint. Meanwhile, he also alerted his hired goons and told them to begin the search for the lost men. Then suddenly,

"Where were you? Thank god you are alive!" Bijoy said when he saw the two Unknowns walking into the ashram.

The men were very tired and in shock. They were not able to speak. Kevin helped them to lie down on the bed and Bijoy sat near one of them.

"What happened? Who were they?" Bijoy asked.

"Arini, the woman from Xiamen triad. They took us and almost killed us but then there was a mysterious girl whom they had kidnapped. She saved our lives," one of the Unknowns replied.

"Mysterious girl?" Bijoy murmured.

"Yes, a mysterious girl. She had seen us being killed by Arini in her dream. She also knows where the Agha Netra is to be found. So, she exchanged our lives with the Agha Netra. And that Arini let us go," one of the Unknowns said.

"What was her name?" Anityo walked into the room to validate the name on his mind.

"Alisha. Her name was Alisha."

Kevin and Sana echoed the name loudly in surprise.

"Alisha?"

Anityo looked at Bijoy.

"I do not want to repeat what happened with Joy. We need to save Alisha from Arini. We need to get her back."

Kevin called Rajat. "Where is Alisha?"

"It's none of your business, Kevin. You have done enough damage to her and unfortunately to me as well," Rajat replied.

"Rajat, listen to me. Alisha is in serious trouble. She has been kidnapped by a triad from Xiamen. I just sent you my location on WhatsApp. Please come down here now!" Kevin pleaded.

"What?" Rajat said in shock. "Hold on, I just dropped her home. How could she be kidnapped? Listen Kevin, if this is a joke then you will be in serious trouble."

"Believe me, Rajat, she is indeed in trouble."

Kevin begged Rajat to come down to Anityo's ashram.

In an hour, Rajat reached the ashram. It was dawn, and the sky was partly coloured orange and the wind was cold.

Rajat went inside and saw Sana standing near the Buddha statue.

"What you are doing here? Where is Alisha?" Rajat went near Sana.

"It's a long story, Rajat. Everything happened so quickly that I did not get time to explain this to Alisha," Sana replied.

Kevin and Sana explained what had happened in the last few weeks and how they were helping a group which was hunting for the Agha Netra. Because of the oath, they did not reveal that they were part of the Nine Unknowns. They told Rajat that they were helping Bijoy.

Anityo overheard Kevin and Sana speaking to Rajat. He looked at Bijoy.

"The sincerity and commitment of Sana and Kevin is commendable. They told Rajat everything but did not reveal the most important secret."

"Anityo, I want to ask you something," Bijoy said. "How did Arini or the triad know we are here? And what do you know about us or Arini?"

Anityo went close to Bijoy and looked into his eyes.

"I was sent here by Xiamen a decade back." Taking a moment, he continued, "In search of the Agha Netra!"

Bijoy was shocked to hear that Anityo had been planted by the Xiamen triad to search for the Agha Netra. That statement shook his belief. Who was Anityo? Did he know everything about the Nine Unknowns?

"Bijoy, this is worrying I know. But Arini saw two of your friends here. And that's it," Anityo said.

The question was still unanswered. Who told her that they were the Unknowns? Who knew that secret about them? Was it Kevin or Sana? Or Anityo?

Bijoy was worried. Whom could he trust now?

It was difficult for Rajat to come to terms with the fact that Alisha had been abducted. And that too by the notorious Xiamen triad.

Rajat muttered, "I know where they might have taken her. I know where the Agha Netra was last spotted."

This statement startled everyone, and their faces displayed a mix of shock and amazement.

They couldn't help but wonder how Rajat had this knowledge about the Agha Netra. The unspoken question hung in the air. Could this be the reason behind Alisha being in the clutches of Arini?

"Where is the Agha Netra?" Bijoy rushed and grabbed Rajat's collar.

Rajat held Bijoy's hands and threw them aside and said in a crying voice, "Where is Alisha?"

"This needs to be solved together, Bijoy. There is no point in fighting each other," said one of the Unknowns to Bijoy in an attempt to calm him down.

Kevin went next to Rajat and said, "Where is the Agha Netra? I mean where was it found last? Alisha will certainly be there with Arini."

Rajat looked at Kevin.

"You are ruthlessly evil, Kevin. You have done enough to get Alisha into trouble. Earlier you impersonated me and now this chapter Arini of Xiamen. Don't you feel ashamed of yourself, Kevin?"

Kevin looked at Sana who had already formed an impression of

Kevin in her mind. And now what Rajat said would only reinforce the impression she already had.

Kevin looked at Rajat.

"I know what I have done is unforgivable. But now we have to save Alisha and the Agha Netra. Let's go and do what is the need of the hour."

Anityo was following the conversation closely. It was time for him to reach out to someone in Xiamen. While Rajat was still talking about the Agha Netra, Anityo went out of the ashram and dialled a number which was on his speed dial.

"They know where it is. I have sent my men to find it before them. If I get it, tell me what will I get back in exchange?"

"The Agha Netra belongs to me. It has always belonged to the heir of Wo Shing Wo. It belongs to his grandson, Sun Yen. That bitch will never get it. You get it for me, and I will bring you back to Xiamen safely."

Anityo smiled and agreed to hand it over to Sun Yen.

Bijoy, Kevin, Sana, Rajat and the Unknowns set out for the cave. They had to reach it before Arini did.

"How many people have you hurt in your life, Kevin?" Sana who was sitting beside Kevin asked in a low voice.

"Sometime, events in life happen for a purpose, Sana. I played many roles in this hunt without any reason. You are here to prove your Baba was right. That letter has a purpose. Alisha is chasing her dream to save a life. Rajat is helping Alisha to find that box and Bijoy is here for his commitment. What I am doing here? I would have left the day I handed over the letter from Bijoy to you. But I am still here, part of this so-called treasure hunt."

Kevin replied looking at the meandering road.

"Then why are you here, Kevin? I was expecting you to leave long ago," Rajat said looking at Kevin.

Sana knew that Kevin was there because Bijoy asked him to join the Unknowns to find and protect the Agha Netra.

"I am here to find and protect something till eternity," Kevin replied.

Bijoy was wondering whether Kevin might reveal his secret of being one of the Unknowns.

"What is that?" Rajat frowned.

Kevin looked at Sana the car's rearview mirror.

"A heart," he replied.

Sana was unaware of what Kevin said when he was looking at her.

Within an hour they reached the entrance of the jungle. Bijoy didn't take much time to realize that they were at the same spot. After walking for a while, they reached at the spot where deodar trees were marked with a cross.

"We have been here before. We've seen these trees and the marks on them."

"Alisha drew these crosses to remember the path. If you were here, it means you were very close to the temple," Rajat said.

Soon after walking around for a couple of hours, they reached the temple which was hidden by the plateau.

Rajat asked them to follow him and they reached the temple underground. It was lit up with a yellow torch and the deity's face was glowing in the yellow warmth.

"This looks like exactly what the letter says. Amazing! It proves that a place which the letter mentions does exist," Kevin said in a low and surprised voice.

Sana was staring at the deity. She folded her hands and closed her eyes.

"Ma, where is my friend? Where is Alisha?"

A loud sound thundered and echoed inside the hollow cave.

"They took her. They were here, and they went back in search of Kingla. That girl can see everything in her dreams, but she can't see Kingla. She will not be able to find it. And she will die one day. All of you will die one day."

The blind saint came down from the stairs near the deity.

Bijoy went up to him.

"Where is the Agha Netra? Where is that box?"

The saint went close to him. "Unknown, I can smell an Unknown. You betrayer! You lost it long back, now it does not belong to you anymore. Agha Netra will find its fate. If the Agha Netra decides that it belongs to the Unknown, you will get it back. It is now up to the Agha Netra to decide which way it will go."

And the saint started to laugh like a maniac.

Rajat went to Bijoy and told him about the Kingla tribe who robbed the cave and took away the box full of weapons. That box had the Agha Netra inside.

"If they couldn't find the box, it means they will kill Alisha," Kevin said worryingly.

"No, they will not. Remember Alisha can dream of things happening in the future. Arini will keep Alisha safe like a treasure," Rajat replied.

"Now the question is where is the Kingla tribe? Where will we find them?" one of the Unknowns asked.

***

Later during that day in the ashram, Anityo called someone.

"You are still blind. How difficult is it?" Anityo laughed.

The voice on the other side of the phone said, "We need to move fast. Two of them have reached here. I managed to misguide them. Anityo, but if they find out who we are, it will all will be over."

"It's like a food chain. While Arini and Bijoy will be busy in a rat race to look for the Agha Netra, a predator will eat those rats." Anityo smiled again.

"Where is that box? Are you sure the Agha Netra is inside?"

"Yes, I am sure. But I want you to open that box. It's safe with me here," the voice said. "But what about the Kinglas? Do they still meet?"

"Yes, I heard they do gather, though only a few have survived."

Anityo hung up the phone and dialled another number.

"Mr Sun Yen, I think the time has arrived to claim your pride... your heir... your throne."

After a brief conversation, Anityo asked, "What I will get in return Sun Yen?"

"You will get your life back, Anityo. Free of the murder charges. You will be treated royally back home," Sun Yen replied.

***

Kamla was sick with worry. What had happened to Alisha? She hadn't come home since the previous evening. In search of her, she met Sana's father, and they both decided to file a missing complaint.

"Nowadays, Sana always comes home late too. Sometime she leaves early in the morning even before dawn. I am worried that these girls might be in some trouble," Sana's father said.

"Alisha was searching for a box lately. I am worried that she may have fallen into wrong hands. They might take her life," cried Kamla sobbing like a baby.

Sana's father pacified Kamla, and they rushed to the police station to file a complaint. On the way she thought of Anityo and decided to meet him and ask him if he could help find Alisha.

They reached Anityo's ashram. Anityo came to the main hall and saw Kamla.

"How are you, Kamla? What brings you here?"

Kamla told Anityo that Alisha was missing.

"This is indeed worrying, Kamla. But you don't worry. Wherever she is, she will be safe. I will also ask people around to help find her," Anityo smiled and asked Kamla to go back home.

Kamla left and after a while Arini walked inside Anityo's house.

"The chest is with me and the saint is dead, Anityo," she giggled while walking inside the house.

Anityo pretended to be surprised.

"Sorry, Arini. I didn't understand. Who is dead?"

"The chest which had weapons is with me, and it does not have the Agha Netra. Where I can find the Kinglas, Anityo? Where are Kinglas nowadays? Who will know better than you?"

Arini smiled looking at Anityo.

"What are you saying Arini? Please come and sit. We can talk," Anityo said.

Arini pulled out a gun and pointed it at Anityo's forehead.

"The Kinglas are an endangered species. If I pull this trigger, they will be almost extinct forever. Whoops and gone!" Arini laughed like a maniac.

After that brief Arini left the place. Anityo immediately called the saint, but no one picked up the phone. He dialled the number continuously. After sometime, a stranger picked up the phone and told Anityo that the owner of the phone was dead.

The saint who met everyone in the cave was dead. And the Agha Netra was not inside the chest. Anityo was in a fix; he promised Sun Yen to come and take it from him. But now Anityo was also clueless about the Agha Netra. *Where was it?*

Arini went back to her house. She walked into the room where Alisha was kept, with her hands tied up.

Alisha looked at her asked, "Who are you?"

Arini frowned, "What did you just ask?"

Alisha was frightened and said in a low voice.

"Sorry I can't recognize you. Who are you?"

Alisha explained that she was face blind. Arini was surprised to hear that. What was the use of dreaming of someone who is going die? When Alisha couldn't even remember their faces? How could she save them?

"Look Alisha, the Agha Netra is lost forever. I don't think we will ever be able to find it now," Arini said in a worried tone.

"I don't think it's the same temple I saw in my dreams," Alisha said pacifying Arini.

Alisha explained her dream. She told Arini everything, even the fact that Kamla has met Saint Anityo and explained Alisha's situation to him. But nothing worked and Alisha situation still remained the same.

Alisha also told Arini that she was not sure whether it was the same temple she had seen in her dream. As she never even remembered going inside the cave. The temple in her dream was above the ground.

"What does that mean?" Arini was surprised.

"Someone learned about my dream, and staged the temple to make me believe that the temple under that plateau is the same temple I saw in my dream," Alisha replied.

Arini shouted, "Anityo, you bastard!"

When Anityo had heard Kamla's story, and had implanted a fake blind saint in the cave. The saint narrated a story taught by Anityo himself. The cave had been staged by Anityo.

***

On the other side of the city, in the jungle, Sana looked at the letter again.

"Those were last lines. We are out of clues now."

Bijoy thought that the Agha Netra was lost forever. They were losing hope and people day by day. And while Arini was in the picture, the fight to find the Agha Netra was proving even more difficult. In all that chaos, one thing that always bothered Bijoy was – who was Arini? How did she know that the Agha Netra was in Mussoorie?

Worried and lost with no way of moving forward, they decided to go to Anityo's ashram and decide what to do next. When they reached there, they saw a girl with Chinese-Indian features walking out of the house.

Kevin went close to Rajat.

"I think she the Arini who Anityo was talking about. If we follow her, she might take us to Alisha."

Rajat looked at the girl and his gut feeling echoed what Kevin told him. Rajat agreed, and they decided to follow the girl. When Arini reached a remote house in a far-off corner of Mussoorie, Rajat and Kevin silently sneaked around the house. What they saw in one room made them happy but worried instantly. Alisha was tied to a chair and seemed to be dozing off.

"I don't think we can get inside the house by ourselves, Rajat. We need a helping hand here. Let me call Bijoy; he will arrange some people to help us. "

Kevin called Bijoy and WhatsApped him his current location. As soon as Bijoy got the information, he called Anityo.

"Anityo, it's good news. We know where Arini is and Alisha too. I need some people who can get Alisha out from Arini's clutches."

"Bijoy, great to hear that Alisha has been found. But do not underestimate Arini. She is sharp and strong. The whole Xiamen gang is here. Let us call the police and ask them to handle it." Anityo was worried.

"Police? We do not have time, Anityo. We need to act fast," Bijoy begged.

"Anityo, tell me one thing, what was Arini doing in your house?" Sana walked towards Anityo as he hung up.

"What Arini? Here? No way," Anityo defended himself.

"Do you know how Rajat and Kevin found out about Alisha? When we were coming here, they saw a girl walking out of your house. With a blind guess that she might be Arini, they followed her and ended up finding Alisha," Sana said grimly.

"What are you saying?" Anityo fumbled.

"What's going on, Anityo? What was Arini doing here? And who is Arini?"

Bijoy was livid, because it was the same Arini who had taken the two Unknowns and almost killed them.

Anityo knew he was caught.

"It's time to tell you guys everything between me and Arini. But before that we need to get Alisha out of there. I can't come with you, Bijoy. But I know few men who will help you. They will be here in a couple of minutes. You save Alisha first, come back and we will talk," Anityo convinced Bijoy.

Bijoy went with the men Anityo had called. They reached Arini's house which was guarded by men in civil dress, wielding guns. The house looked like any normal house with lights switched on in a few rooms. There was a simply dressed security guard at the gate.

Bijoy decided to meet Rajat and Kevin, and then the three could sneak into the house quietly. Then Bijoy decided to drop the plan and enter the house like a guest. Taking on the men in the house could be avoided if they could trick them and steal Alisha from under their noses.

He went to the guard and introduced himself as a Xiamen man. He insisted that he had some news for Arini. At first the guard hesitated, saying that there was no one called Arini inside. However, a while later, he allowed Bijoy and the others to go in.

They walked through the gravel path lit by lamps and entered the main hall. The plan he had in mind was that Bijoy and Sana would engage Arini in a conversation. Meanwhile Rajat and Kevin would sneak into the room and get Alisha out. But the whole plan was quashed when Arini walked into the hall.

"Welcome, Bijoy."

Bijoy was shocked when he heard his name.

"Don't be shocked. I know everything about the Unknowns. The group that has lost the Agha Netra, and their pride long back. And now, geared up to find the lost treasure here in Mussoorie," Arini continued.

Bijoy sat on the sofa and looked at her.

"Who are you? How you know about us? How you know we are hunting for the Agha Netra and that it is here in Mussoorie," Bijoy was fumbling.

"Rapid-fire questions," Arini laughed loudly.

"I know you very well. Sun Yen also knows you very well. Now let me answer all your questions in a few words."

"Arinjay, I am the granddaughter of Arinjay. 'Arini', my name, comes from the first few letters of Arinjay, my grandfather. And Sun Yen, that poor little guy, is the grandson of Wo Shing Wo," she smiled.

The name Arinjay sent a shock wave to Bijoy's ears. His blood boiled when he heard that name.

"Arinjay, that traitor!" Bijoy murmured.

"No, that word 'traitor' I don't like. My grandfather was not a traitor, but a loyal man. What he did not get in his whole life, I will get by conquering the throne of the Xiamen triad. The bet is in place. The Agha Netra has to be found."

Arini looked at Bijoy.

Bijoy was adamant that Arinjay was a traitor. The only part which Arini was not ready to accept.

Arini explained to Bijoy that Arinjay decided to hide the Agha Netra before going to Xiamen. He was as loyal as his father Eravanth. But Arinjay's mother was not happy with the poverty-stricken life they lived. She hated the Unknowns to the core. When Arinjay was in Xiamen, he made a duplicate box and took it with him. He knew when he reached Xiamen, the triad would hunt him down and would try to steal the Agha Netra. But before that could have happened Arinjay's mother told the triad about the Agha Netra. Arinjay's mother never knew that it was a duplicate box. So Arinjay left his mother in Xiamen and went to Guangzhou. Later, he married Jia whom he met in the bus. Jia was the daughter of a triad of Guangzhou.

In Xiamen, the triad found out that the Agha Netra was an empty box. They knew that Arinjay had left the original Agha Netra in Mussoorie. Arinjay told Arini the story on his deathbed. Xiamen wanted to give the throne to Sun Yen, but she challenged him. The challenged was whosoever would bring the Agha Netra back would lead the triad. The Guangzhous wanted to expand their region, and she was helping them.

"It's a long story, isn't it, Bijoy? Now you stop calling my grandfather a traitor. He served his loyalty with whatever means he could."

"Yes, he was not a traitor. The Unknowns will learn the truth. But why do you need the Agha Netra? The Agha Netra is our faith… our reason to live. And you need the Agha Netra to conquer the throne. What happens after that?" Bijoy was firm in his response.

"After that, it's a piece of box for me or a souvenir. But for now, it's the key to lead the Xiamen triad," Arini replied.

"Arini, I know I should not say this. But I will say it, anyway. We can help each other in this hunt. Once we get the Agha Netra, you go to Xiamen with it and prove that you are ready to lead the throne," Bijoy walked to Arini and whispered in her ears.

"After you get your throne, hand over the Agha Netra back to us. We will protect it as we promised," Bijoy looked at Arini and smiled.

Bijoy convinced Arini that they had a letter written by Sana's Baba with a map leading to the Agha Netra. If she promised Bijoy that she'd hand over the Agha Netra to the unknowns and free Alisha, together they'd be able to get to the Agha Netra sooner.

Arini knew that they did not find anything in that cave. So, this battle of finding Agha Netra would be better fought together. She had also got a tip-off that Sun Yen might be in town anytime to join the hunt for the Agha Netra.

"Bijoy, I know when you stick to your promise, you fulfil it. But if in case I smell a betrayal, then this small group of yours will be erased in a jiffy."

Arini walked up to Bijoy

"Let's work together."

And she signalled her men to release Alisha.

Bijoy did what Namish Sarkar had done to Arinjay. Handing over the Agha Netra to be protected. He gambled the hunt, and the bet was the Agha Netra.

While Bijoy was walking out of the hall, he paused. He turned back and asked Arini, "Did Anityo know about us? Did he know who the Unknowns are?".

"Yes" Arini smiled.

In the next few minutes, she elaborated Anityo's past. As Bijoy listened to her, the veil from Anityo's face was coming off, revealing who he truly was.

They all reached Anityo's ashram to find that the ashram was deserted. Anityo had left the place with his men. He knew that Bijoy would not spare him once he came to know his reality from Arini.

The search was about to start again. One thing was clear: what Alisha saw in her dreams and what was described in the letter was not the hollow cave structure but a temple above the surface. So, the question still remained to be solved. Where was the temple?

The search started again. They decided to connect the dots all over again. The dream, the letter and whatever leads they had. They had to look at everything with a fresh perspective. Alisha narrated what she had seen in the dream – running through the deodar trees, she tumbled at once place, where she saw a temple. She got up and found herself inside the temple.

What Sana's Baba wrote in the letter which when decoded, was a temple too. A kali temple, aloof in the jungle, in the shape of a hut with a spear on top.

While all this was happening, something struck Sana, and she told everyone about the Devalsari temple. She argued that there was a similar temple in a jungle. It was always filled with devotees. She told them to take a chance, and see if they were talking about the same temple.

It seemed improbable as Devalsari was a known temple now. What was the possibility of the box still being there? However, in that situation, they didn't have any other option.

They started to follow a narrow and winding path through a dense deodar forest. The sunlight filtered through the leaves, creating a magical and peaceful atmosphere. Finally, after a few hours of walking, they reached the Devalsari temple. It was more beautiful than they had imagined, with intricate carvings and a sense of divine calm.

"Let's go in and see if we can find something," Kevin said to Bijoy.

"I don't believe that it will still be there. Did you see the same temple in your dream?" Rajat asked Alsiha.

"I am not sure, it looks familiar though," Alisha replied.

Kevin went in and Rajat followed. It was crowded with devotees standing outside the temple. The temple was closed. They peeped through the windows and tried to look inside the temple. A pujari saw them.

"What you want?"

Kevin asked, "When it will open?"

"In April. What do you want?"

"We are looking for a box. Is there a big box like a chest inside the temple? It was kept years ago," Rajat said.

"No there is no such box inside. Even if there would have been one, the Kinglas would have taken it long ago," the pujari smiled and went back.

"Where I can find the Kingla tribe?" Bijoy asked.

"The tribe was active at the time of India's independence. They were so notorious that they even looted the British for weapons and money. Later in the eighties and nineties, they merged back into civil society. If you know anyone living a civil life and belonging to the Kingla tribe, they will tell you if the tribe has stolen the box. There are still a few who meet regularly and secretly keep their tradition alive. What I know so far is that there is a hidden temple and a book they worship."

Devlsari was not the temple they were looking for. And, there was no light at the end of that tunnel.

They all sat near the temple. Once again, they were directionless. Finding the Kingla tribe was a new piece in the jigsaw puzzle.

"Are we talking about a real box here? Does the Agha Netra even exist?" Kevin was frustrated and asked Bijoy.

"You know very well, Kevin, it is there somewhere. Our existence itself is living evidence that it exists. We lost it long back. And this hunt is to find it again."

Bijoy was confident.

The question of existence twitched thoughts in the minds of those who joined the hunt very recently. They did not find any iota of evidence that it existed apart from a dream, a letter, and the Unknowns. But the Agha Netra did exist. Otherwise, Xiamen would not have got involved in the hunt for the throne. Everyone has a reason to believe that it is there, somewhere. They all hooked their hopes on the Kinglas, the erstwhile notorious tribe.

All of a sudden, Rajat felt a sense of déjà vu when he heard the name. He had heard that name somewhere before. And then he remembered Joy, the librarian. He did mention a tribe like the Kinglas, and that there were some books about it in the library.

"I have heard this name of the tribe before. I think we might be able to get some information about them in the library," Rajat told the others.

"Do you think we'll be able to find something in the big library?" Sana asked.

"Yes. I know the staff there who can help us," Rajat responded.

They decided that the next day Bijoy, Rajat and Kevin would go to library.

From that temple, Kevin dropped everyone home. In the sequence Sana was the last one to reach home.

Kevin reached Sana's house and waited for her to get down from the car.

"You're home," Kevin told Sana.

"Why are you with us, Kevin? Why did you join the Unknowns? Each one of us has some purpose to find the Agha Netra. But what purpose do you have?" Sana questioned him.

"I don't think that you are ready to believe me, Sana. But one day, you will understand," Kevin replied solemnlv.

"I hope that day come will soon, Kevin. You were a mystery to me when we first met, and you are a mystery even now," Sana replied and got down from the car.

Kevin said to himself watching Sana walk past the gate, "Sometimes, you always have to prove your love even though the one you love, never sees its true value. Love needs sacrifices. And yes, pain."

***

The next day Kevin, Rajat and Bijoy were in the library flipping through few articles about the Kinglas. There was some connection of the Kingla tribe to a village called Kangal village from where they got their name. It indicated that almost anyone who was born in this village were part of the Kingla tribe. But while India was getting united, this village merged with other surrounding villages and mysteriously vanished from the India map. The location which was mentioned was not far from Mussoorie. This indicated that if the Kinglas kept their tradition alive to gather secretly, they must be around somewhere Mussoorie.

"I know someone whose family was from Kangal," Bijoy stated.

"Who is that?" Rajat and Kevin asked in unison.

"Our dear Anityo. He told me one once jokingly that his parents were born in a place that doesn't even exist on India's map. I will not be surprised if he is one from the current generation of the tribe," Bijoy said with frowning.

"And he is gone with all his men," Kevin said.

"The mystery is why he did he suddenly leave the ashram? Did he know that we were behind the Agha Netra? But even in that case, why would he leave the ashram?" Rajat said.

"If I am not wrong, they might meet at the place where we found the deity statue in the cave. He knew we will find that cave and he made us believe that the Agha Netra was stolen by the Kinglas," Bijoy surmised.

"Even if Anityo is from Kingla, he doesn't know that someone from his tribe has the Agha Netra. Else it would have gone with him forever," Kevin said.

Bijoy was still not able to accept that a saint who was living a by the teachings of Buddha, had such a criminal past. In addition, the Kinglas merged with the society leaving all the sins behind. If Anityo was one of them, why he did he go to Xiamen? What was Anityo's story?

The trio at the library dug deeper into numerous books and Google searches and stumbled upon a specific pattern about the Kinglas. The tribe had looted Englishmen during British the succession. This included gold, artifacts, money, and weapons. Soon after independence, the Kingla tribes merged into civil society. They were rich people due to inherited looted wealth. At some point in time, they realized that they were losing their name. They wanted to retain the soul of the tribe but, this time, give something back to society. So, they formed a secret group. A secret society.

Society has a process for introducing new people, but the reins of control remain with the few. The original Kingla generation. The tribe meets at some secret place to continue the tradition of paying homage to the departed soul. Being devotees of Ma Kali, it's a hidden temple somewhere where the rituals take place.

Given the limited information about the Kinglas in the library, that's all they could find. The information about the Kinglas meeting at the Kali temple was in the same line as the clue they found in Baba's letter and Alisha's dream.

The pointers indicated that the Kinglas also had something to do with the Agha Netra. Bijoy decided they must find Anityo, who would have a clue about this secret society. They had to find the saint who mocked being a monk. Anityo was their last hope.

Bijoy decided to split the group into two, one that'd go to the ashram and other to the temple they found in the plateau. Whoever found Anityo would inform the other immediately.

Alisha, Rajat, Sana and Kevin were the ones who went to the ashram, while Bijoy and Arini headed to the plateau. The two weaker Unknowns were left behind to rest.

Alishas' group reached the ashram with the hope that Anityo would return soon.

"How I will recognize him if he just walks into this house? Can anyone tell me a particular thing about Anityo?" Alisha was worried.

"I will make one on his face if he walks into the house," Kevin replied furiously.

"The same way you got one near Gully's cafe, and that helped Alisha to recognize you as Rajat," Sana smirked.

"I was the one responsible for that. One of the grave mistakes I committed in my life," Rajat said looking at Sana.

At the moment, all the three pairs of eyes were staring at Kevin. Kevin was disheartened. He was losing hope of finding the Agha Netra, losing hope to regain his lost friend, and losing hope that Sana would understand his untold love for her one day.

A broken heart never really heals; it just learns to live in pieces.

A numb Kevin came out of the ashram and sat on the bench in the garden. Remembering his past, a loner living in Kolkata's old streets. How things changed his life in the last few months. Born with dyslexia, Kevin learned how to decipher messages from images and words.

While he was strolling down memory lane, a hazy figure walked past in front of him. He looked at him casually and then his eyes frowned. Anityo was back in the ashram.

Anityo unaware that Rajat, Alisha and Sana were waiting inside, walked in front of the Buddha in lotus position.

After a few minutes, a voice knifed the silence, "Welcome home, Anityo."

Anityo partially in shock turned around and saw the trio standing just behind him, while Kevin walked in speaking on the phone. He called Bijoy.

"He is in the ashram; you guys come over."

"I thought you all left in search of the Agha Netra. I don't have any clue where it is. What are you guys are doing here?" Anityo said in a shaking voice.

"Tell me one thing, Anityo, do you know who are the Kinglas? And are you connected in any way to them?" Rajat asked.

Anityo knew he would be asked about his past one day. The past from which he had been running away since ages. Now Anityo was tired of running. He did what was best in his capacity – to stay away from his identity, but now he was losing his will power. The questions stung Anityo like a bee and he was ready to let people know who Anityo really was.

"The Kinglas are no more, they gave up arms and violence, and they took an oath in front of Ma Kali and they all dispersed into normal life. None of them surrendered with weapons but promised themselves that it was time to give back to society. The famous businessman in Mussoorie, Singhania also descended from the Kingla tribe.

"Once the Kingla tribe dissolved, they formed a secret society. This society was formed to remind them of a promise they made. Never to pick up weapons and violence. But I was a traitor, a murderer, and an undeterred lover, who loved someone relentlessly."

Anityo paused briefly.

"I was a member of the secret society who is now running away from them to save himself."

Bijoy walked into the house and looked at Anityo.

"You sold us, Anityo. Who else knows we are here?"

"The Xiamen triad, contender of the crown, Mr Who also knows that you are here. I traded my life for the Agha Netra," Anityo replied.

Alisha approached Anityo, curiously, "How do we find the Kinglas? Where's the secret society? Tell me your story, Anityo. Who are you?"

Anityo moved to a nearby sofa and said, "I will tell you everything about the Kinglas and how you can find the secret society."

All eyes were on him as he was about to reveal the most unknown part of the search – the Kinglas.

Chapter 23

The Last Resort

During the freedom struggle, the Kinglas realized that looting Englishmen was justified because, unknowingly and indirectly, the Kinglas were helping the fight for freedom. But after independence, a section of the Kinglas felt it was wrong to steal and loot from Indians who had fought for independence. They thought it was a sin to loot their own people. So, they decided it was time to talk to their leader and ask him to stop looting and stealing, and enjoy the fresh air of freedom with their fellow men. Little did they know that Shambhu, then leader of the Kinglas wouldn't agree easily. He was used to living a luxurious life, and giving it up wouldn't be something he'd do without a fight.

However, while the Englishmen were handing over the power to the local jurisdiction after independence, they also handed over the case of the Kinglas. It was not a normal for two powers to unite for one cause – to nab the Kinglas one day.

The Indian police decided to keep their hunt on to bring down the notorious tribe. And for that reason, security was strengthened to such an extent that once the informer, who were giving tips against the Englishmen, were now providing clues to them to hunt down the Kinglas.

"'Our tribe is best known for snatching wealth from people who have more than what they need. We are always successful because we were blessed by Ma Kali. If we were not doing something right, then we would not have earned so much of wealth.' Shambu said to the Kingla tribesmen who went to convince him.

Shambhu, a man with a towering presence reflected strength and authority. With each word he spoke, he commanded attention, his oratory skills weaving tales of inspiration and leadership, igniting flames of passion in the hearts of all who listened.

Listening to him, they returned with the belief that even in independent India, looting and banditry were justified. However, only a handful within the Kinglas were aware that persuading Shambhu to abandon this path wouldn't be a simple task. They were also aware of Shambhu's strong superstitions, realizing that if they could somehow convince him that pursuing a life of crime was detrimental to his future, he might change one day.

The enlightened ones in the Kinglas knew what to do in this situation. And what they were best at. They opted for a patient approach, waiting for the right moment to persuade Shambhu. This group, which was now a rebel force inside the Kinglas consisted of only a handful. They knew that looting their own people was not going to serve any good. So, instead of taking any drastic step against Shambu, they agreed to convince him with superstition rather than force.

The Kinglas continued the tradition of meeting at Ma Kali's temple before they were to go on a loot. Here at the temple, they always reminded each other that they were born for this purpose and were ready to die. During the period when India was celebrating its independence they were at the job, primarily looting Englishmen who were leaving the country.

The security was becoming stricter, people were openly supporting the local police, giving tips in case anyone had any clue about the Kinglas. It was not easy for the Kinglas to move around. Or find someone to loot so easily.

That evening, the tribe came back from hunting without any catch. Shambhu decided they should spend the night in the jungle instead of going home empty-handed. They would try again the next day. Since they hadn't exerted themselves while looting or dacoity, they weren't tired. Some members, unable to sleep, roamed around and stumbled upon a temple nestled deep within the quiet jungle. The presence of a temple in such a remote location seemed unbelievable. They thought it was an abandoned temple that no one would be taking care of. Yet, when they entered, they were surprised to find it immaculately clean and well-maintained, defying all expectations.

In the hope that they might get something valuable in the temple, they started searching haphazardly. There was a secret door which took them down through a staircase. The temple was well ventilated, but the air around the stairs and the rabbit hole emitted a musty odour. The smell reminded them of mould and decay, lingering in the air and sticking to everything. It made the place feel ancient and forgotten, like nobody had stepped there in a long time. Despite the good ventilation, the odour was strong, making them aware of the age and neglect of the place.

"Looks like some secret place. Might be a tunnel that leads to something. Shall we go in?" the one standing at the entrance of the door said.

"Anyway, we do not have anything to do. At least, we will make use of our time. Let's light the torch and go in," said another.

That place spooked them and gave a feeling of something wasn't right. However, it was greed that motivated them. In case they found anything of value, it would enough to please the frustrated boss sitting outside in the jungle. With that hope, a few of them went inside.

While going down, the smell got stronger and stronger. They were removing the thick spiderwebs with the help of the dim yellow light of the torch that easily showed them the thickness of dust on the surface. Suddenly, in that gloomy room something glittered. A chest, with a golden strap beautifully woven around its border, lay in the middle of the chamber.

They had hit a jackpot.

It was a heavy box. It was so heavy that the strong six-footed men, who possessed formidable bodies with muscles honed through years of relentless training and physical labour, were unable to bring it up. Just by the weight of the box, they were certain that they had found something of worth.

Finally, after hours of work, they managed to haul it out of the temple.

"What have you found?" Shambhu said, smiling at the box.

"It must be some treasure hidden inside the temple, Shambhu. The sheer weight can tell us how much wealth there is stored," the man replied panting.

"What are we waiting for? Quickly open the chest."

Shambhu was excited.

To their surprise, as they opened the lid of the chest, it was filled with weapons. There was also a mysterious object in the box. Shambhu picked up the mysterious object and laughed.

While he was holding the box, the loud sound of gunfire pierced the stillness, and one of his men fell on the ground.

The Indian police along with some Englishmen had found the Kinglas in the jungle. The only thing the Kinglas could do was to leave the heavy chest behind and run away to save their lives.

But someone shouted at Shambhu.

"The chest has weapons and we can fight back."

Shambhu holding the mysterious box in one hand, picked up a firearm and started shooting the policemen. The others picked up the weapons in the chest and gave a befitting reply to the police.

They fought with full strength and managed to flee.

During this encounter with the police, Shambu was badly hurt. The majority of his men had died in the encounter, but he survived holding the mysterious box.

"See Shambhu, it is because of this box that you are alive. Look at the bodies around yourself. We don't have enough men to even carry out the final rituals of the dead," a survivor cried.

"This is a sign sent by Ma Kali that we need to give up this business of looting people. This box you are holding is our saviour," he added.

Shambhu who had just cheated death believed him.

That night the tribe returned, disappointed, broken and hurt, and with less than half of the men alive.

"It's a big loss for the Kinglas, and I know it's hard to recover from the loss. It is time we go back to the people and live with them. The Kinglas should be dissolved and should merge back into the society," Shambhu said.

"We have looted them for long, and now it's time to give back. Let us promise today that we all will go back and help people as much as we can."

It was certainly a change of heart for Shambhu. The Kinglas formally gave up their notorious business of looting people. However, they did not surrender.

After a year of the Kinglas being dissolved, a few decided to form a secret society. Shambhu who was still the unspoken leader due to the respect he held, agreed. And the mysterious object became a pious relic of the secret society. A symbol that united the members of the secret society.

Now the importance of the mysterious object, was equivalent to the god's gift. As part of the tradition, the Kinglas decided to keep the object in the locker, only to be brought out twice every year.

Anityo was born in one of the families in the secret society. He knew that there was a mysterious object the members of the society pray to. Anityo was not religious since birth and he always felt that the relic helped to keep the people of the secret society united. As far as Anityo's inclination to see and observe the mysterious object went, he had seen it from afar, and never had any curiosity to study the object up close.

Anityo as any other normal teen, grew within the society, following its rules. Which was work hard for oneself and share the success with the people. Exactly the reason why the Kinglas were merged back into civil society. Giving back to society and sharing any success with them. Anityo soon he fell in love. The girl was not from the secret society. As the years passed by, the rules of the secret society became stricter. The inclusion of anyone from outside needed a vote by the board of the secret society, that would approve and endorse the induction.

Anityo knew he wouldn't get those votes so easily. Slowly as his love become passionate and serious, this dedication and passion bought Anityo in front of the board to beg for his love's inclusion as a member.

"You know that it's impossible to convince the members," Anityo's father, a businessman, said in an attempt to convince him.

"In that case I will leave the society. What is the purpose of this society when I can't live with the love of my life? We have been taught to give back to society, then what is the harm to get someone inducted into our society. Slowly, I feel like we have become godlike for people, and we feel so superior that others can't be part of us." Anityo was frustrated.

"Anityo, I think you should take a break. There is a business opportunity in Xiamen. The deal is waiting for our nod. You just go and see them. If you are convinced, feel free to take the call. This travel will not only give you a break from the daily routine, but will give you an opportunity to think twice about your decision to marry the girl you love."

His father slapped his shoulder and walked away.

Half convinced, Anityo decided that he would make at least one attempt from his heart to meet the members of the board and seek their approval.

"Since the inception of this society, we have always supported the people in the outside world. Given the way we work, it would be difficult to believe that someone new will work with the same faith," one of the members said.

"We see you as our next board member, Anityo. You have the capability to be part of the group," another said.

"Listen to your father and take a break, Anityo, come back and vet your decision again," one of the members replied.

Amidst all the rejection, Anityo decided that he would travel to Xiamen and think of how to stay with the girl he loved.

After a couple of days, Anityo, with two other members of the board, reached Xiamen. In a week the deal was closed and they were preparing to come back.

"So, what you have decided, Anityo? I would say, leave that girl. Don't complicate life for both worlds," a member said.

"I am not making life complicated; I am setting up an example for all the other secret society members that they are free to love whomever they want," Anityo said.

"What is so interesting about that girl, Anityo, that gave you so much courage to rebel?"

"It doesn't matter who is she, it's all about how much you love her. And love is the fuel that ignites the fire of courage in your heart, empowering you to confront your fears," Anityo said.

Anityo was not comfortable discussing his situation with the men.

"This has created a serious impact on your mental health. Leave her for the betterment of the secret society. Even if she comes with us, no one will accept her," another gave his unsolicited advice.

Anityo lost his cool after numerous personal attacks. He picked up a ceramic vase and smashed it on the member's head. It was a brutal hit that brought him to the ground. He was dead.

Anityo has just killed the son of the founding member of the secret society.

The second member who had witnessed the scene called the police and stood near the dead body.

Anityo managed scoot from the place and hid in a hotel in Guangzhou. The Guangzhou triad came to know about Anityo's deed and found him out in the hotel.

"Hi Anityo, I am Arini. I know what you have done. And now you are a phone call away from imprisonment." Arini smiled.

"Don't worry we can be of your help and you can be of ours. Shall I tell you about the deal?" she continued.

Anityo was still in shock at his unintentional crime. He quickly agreed, hoping she would help him out. Arini told Anityo to go to a place in India called Mussoorie and find out all he could about the Agha Netra which was a brown mysterious box, with an eye engraved on it.

Since that horrific incident, he was in Mussoorie living a disguised life of a monk. But always under the radar of Arini, who was patiently waiting for Anityo to find the Agha Netra.

Chapter 24

A Secret Society

Everyone was silent when they heard Anityo's story.

"So, how we can reach out to the secret society?" Alisha asked curiously.

"The mysterious object that they worship will be for display soon for all the society members at a secret festival. However, we can't go to the festival because we are not part of it," Anityo said.

"But aren't you still part of the same society?" Kevin responded.

"And you think I will step on the last mile, to hasten to the gallows?" Anityo replied.

"Look Anityo, this hunt means a lot to us. You ran away from your love, you disrespected the society and now, by not supporting us, you are again losing an opportunity to show your worth," Alisha tried to persuade Anityo.

"Let me place my bet on this. You take us to the object and let us see it, and I promise to bring it back from them safely," Arini said as she walked up to Anityo and kept her hand on his shoulder.

Anityo was not convinced, but he was not left with much of a choice.

"The rituals to put up that object for display will start in the next two days. It will be on display for a week. I know where they will meet and can take you there," Anityo said quietly. We will have to get this made on your hand. It will serve like a passport for the rituals."

He pulled up his left sleeve and showed them a tattoo.

The dawn next morning bought hope to the group who were sure the mysterious object of the tribe must be the Agha Netra they were looking for.

"How we will recognize the Agha Netra even if it is kept in front of us? Have anyone of us has seen it?" Kevin asked.

"The image that we have in our mind is a clear picture. That should not be difficult," Bijoy replied.

The road to reach the secret society was not less than an expedition through the deep deodar forests. Anityo was navigating quickly through the trees. Clearly, he knew the path by heart. The thirst for the object and the thinning patience had pumped so much stamina into the group that even the older ones were not resting. They were restless souls on a mission.

After a long walk through the jungle, the group reached a mansion in the middle of the jungle. Secluded and far away from city lights, the palace was guarded by the people in black cloaks. They were more than six feet tall and muscular. The people seeking entry had to show the tattoos on their wrists.

Anityo stopped around a hundred metres away from the mansion and told everyone that they could definitely go close to view the relic. They would have to guess if it was what they were looking for.

Binding all hope, faith and belief with prayers, they walked in one by one. Bijoy was leading the pack in the line. He went inside the mansion and as he stepped inside, he found himself in a big hall split into two parts. On his right there were chairs where few people were sitting looking at the object. These people were facing a big hollow space, curved like a dome at the top. Just below was a hut-shaped temple with a spire that rose symmetrically above the centre. The wall of the temple like structure had a big painting of Ma Kali in gold, and in front of it an object placed vertically, facing the people sitting on the bench.

Bijoy began to feel a strange sensation as he drew closer to the object. He started to feel cold as if he was being connected to a supernatural object or a cosmic phenomenon. He felt that he was being touched by his ancestors who left the earth, or perhaps the Unknowns who had protected the Agha Netra once. It was a deep sense of being in the presence of something greater than oneself.

Bijoy reached close to the relic and looked at it. His eye sparkled and his heart stopped for a while. *The Agha Netra was finally found.*

While he was feeling the presence of the blessing, he heard a thud. He turned to see that Alisha had fallen on the floor. She looked at Bijoy's eyes. The tears in Bijoy eyes were enough to tell her that her dreams had finally culminated. Alisha looked towards left and saw the Kali temple. A red hue was being emitted from the object signifying it was indeed the Agha Netra.

Bijoy went down on his knees, immediately followed by the rest of the other Unknowns. Sana and Kevin looked at the Unknowns and then at each other. After a few seconds, they joined the group.

The Agha Netra was looking down at the seven Unknowns including the messenger who finally found it.

"It has to come back rightfully to our hands. It should be with us."

Bijoy was anxious and happy.

"What should we do now?" Rajat asked.

"There will be a heist!" Arini replied.

There was no other alternative to get the Agha Netra back. They planned to steal the Agha Netra from the mansion that night. Arini started to gather her men. The mansion was standing aloof and isolated in the jungle which was in itself partially protected it from any invasion or theft. This location made the security guards complacent to any threat. Bijoy and the others were aware of it and needed to use it to their advantage.

That night Anityo walked into the mansion, quietly, wearing a black cloak and sneaking through the small gate which led to a dimly lit tunnel. After walking for about fifty metres inside the tunnel, he knocked at a door.

A tall figure opened the door. Anityo without saying a word, walked inside.

"Everyone here?" Anityo stepped inside the room and spoke to all the seven people in the room.

"I hope it's going to be as easy as a mouse taking cheese from a house without a cat."

Everyone in the room nodded. He was talking to all the guards who were in charge of protecting the Agha Netra in the mansion.

"You have been so loyal to me. After a few weeks, a time will come when I will rule this secret society and you will be my close aids."

Everyone in the room giggled.

One of the guards walked down to Anityo and asked,

"Why you are doing this, Anityo? What you will gain out of it? And you know that the relic is a gift from God to us. We are only letting you steal it because one day we will get it back safely," the worried guard asked.

"That relic is godly to me too. I will not lead the secret society unless I have it in my hand and prove I can protect it. After it is stolen today, it will only travel to one place which I know and from there it'll be very easy to get it back." Anityo smiled.

"But why you are doing it?" the guard continued.

"This secret society has never cared of its own people. I lost my love. The one whom I loved so much. She killed herself, just because this society never wanted to accept her. I was in exile for a decade. My family abandoned me. I was treated like crap. This is an opportunity to let the people of this secret society to learn to have a heart so that no Anityo is ever born again," Anityo said with passion. "I am here to change the rule of the game. Forever!"

***

That night in the mansion, Rajat and Kevin went from the front to see who was on guard. Arini and Bijoy were proceeding from the back with a few men. It was surprising as there was no one there. It was completely dark and quiet.

Bijoy reached the door. To his shock it was open. They walked inside the mansion and there were no security guards to be seen. What was going on?

"I think it's a trap, how come no one is around to protect it?" Bijoy said worryingly.

From the front door, Kevin and Rajat walked inside the hall.

They all gathered in front of the Agha Netra. Not a single guard was there to protect it.

"What's happening here?" Rajat was surprised.

"It doesn't matter, let's take it away now," Kevin said, and they all looked at the Agha Netra.

The red hue of the Agha Netra was glowing in the dark creating a mysterious and hypnotic halo.

Bijoy climbed on the platform and took out the Agha Netra which was kept in the box. His hand went cold and his soul felt the calmness that he had been searching for since ages. They swiftly walked outside the mansion.

***

Alisha was worried as she knew someone would hold the box in blood-drenched hands. So far she had seen people die, and she was expecting the same. The question that worried her the most was: Who would be the unlucky one?

While Bijoy was walking back, he gave the Agha Netra to one of the Unknowns.

Anityo who was in mansion walked inside the main hall. He laid his eyes on the empty space where the Agha Netra was previously kept.

The Agha Netra had been stolen from the secret society. Anityo looked at the empty space with a ghostly smile and suddenly his face changed into one of anger.

The next day there was chaos in the secret society when they discovered that the Agha Netra was gone. Everyone thought that the devil had cast its shadow on the society which might break them apart forever.

That day, Anityo walked confidently in the office where the top members of society were having a serious discussion about what to do next.

"I know who stole it. And I can get it back," Anityo said with a smile.

Few days later, Bijoy went to Arini and handed the box to her.

"Here it is, Arini. It has come full circle. A century back, a messenger had handed this over to your grandfather, Arinjay. And today I am handing this over to you. That time there was a promise that Arinjay was asked to keep, and today also I am asking you keep your promise," Bijoy said solemnly.

"I am his granddaughter, Bijoy, and like Arinjay, my loyalty towards the Unknowns remains as pure as my grandfather." Arini paused. "You can trust me."

After a few days, Arini reached Xiamen and claimed her throne to lead the triad. Sun Yen, lost the battle, but he knew what to do next.

"It's with her. It will be a war between triad to get it back," Sun Yen called Anityo.

"Wait for my instructions, I need to convince the secret society members here," Anityo said and hung up.

Anityo went to the members of the board.

"I have finally found where it is. Either you accept my wish to let me lead the secret society or I will be gone forever and so will the relic. The choice is yours."

"You are blackmailing us now?" the members asked in anger.

Anityo walked up to him and said, "You have not left any other choice for me. I was no one for the society a decade back, you treated me like thrash. Now, the tables have turned and I am placing my bet. Take it or leave it!"

A society without the relic felt most vulnerable, and he had no choice but to accept Anityo's demand.

***

The next day, a flight landed at Kolkata airport. A woman holding a blue rucksack walked out of the airport. The taxi reached Sarkar's bungalow, on the eastern side of Kolkata. She walked up to the door and Bijoy opened it. He was surprised and happy to see the much-awaited visitor.

"I knew you will be back, Arini!" Bijoy exclaimed.

"Here it is. Hope you don't find any other Arinjay. Because, I can't guarantee a loyal granddaughter like me." Both of them laughed.

Bijoy knew that they were still seven. It was time to complete the group of nine. He knew that young blood like Rajat and Alisha could fulfil the promise. He convinced them to join the Nine Unknowns. They happily agreed. The hunt for the Agha Netra had bought Rajat and Alisha closure, and the legacy of protecting it from the world was a privilege.

Rajat met the college board to convince them again that the case was in his hand and he would win it any cost. To his surprise the men told him that dispute was over and the brother had agreed to sell the land to the college. The case was closed without any further trial.

Kevin met Rajat in Mussoorie to say a final goodbye.

"Sorry for what I have done, Rajat. And, I would like to confess one more thing that you should know. I planted the story of the evil eye in the affidavit through Shivpal so that you could also get engaged in this case. I was feeling alone while hunting for the Agha Netra and I needed you."

"I would hate to get a friend like you, Kevin. But look at our destiny, you are also an Unknown now to protect the Agha Netra," Rajat smirked.

Bijoy got know that the Xiamen triad were having a gang war to get the Agha Netra, so he decided to hand over the Agha Netra to someone among the Unknowns.

***

After a few days, Alisha heard a knock on the door. As she opened the door, she saw Bijoy standing there, whom she didn't recognize by face.

She gave a puzzled look.

"Who are you?"

Bijoy knew Alisha's condition.

"Protect the Agha Netra, Alisha. You are its guardian now. Prove your loyalty," he said smiling.

Alisha looked at the box and the voice of the man reminded her of Bijoy. She held the box in her hand with pride. But suddenly the biggest worry flashed in her mind.

A part of her dream was yet to come true. She still needed to see a pair of hands soaked in blood holding the Agha Netra.

The Agha Netra was now with a protector who would never remember any faces. For her, the Unknowns would always remain unknowns.